MANHUNT

Also by Wayne Barton & Stan Williams in Large Print:

Live by the Gun

Books by Wayne Barton:

Return to Phantom Hill
Ride Down the Wind

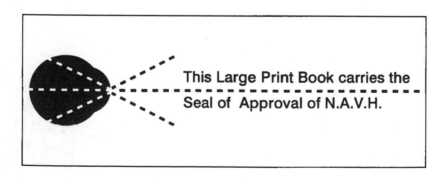

This Large Print Book carries the
Seal of Approval of N.A.V.H.

MANHUNT

WAYNE BARTON
&
STAN WILLIAMS

G.K. Hall & Co.
Thorndike, Maine

Published in 1997 by arrangement with DHS Literary Inc.

G.K. Hall Large Print Western Collection.

The text of this Large Print edition is unabridged.
Other aspects of the book may vary from the original edition.

Set in 16 pt. Plantin by Rick Gundberg.

Printed in the United States on permanent paper.

Library of Congress Cataloging in Publication Data

Barton, Wayne.
   Manhunt / Wayne Barton & Stan Williams.
     p.   cm.
   ISBN 0-7838-8305-6 (lg. print : hc : alk. paper)
   1. Large type books. I. Williams, Stan. II. Title.
  [PS3552.A777M36   1997]
   813'.54-dc21
                                            97-30531

To Jill
for everything,

and

To Bob
who knows what brothers are for.

Authors' Note

On November 19, 1894, Sheriff Andrew J. Royal of Pecos County, Texas, was killed by a shotgun blast while writing his reports in his office in the county court house. His murder ended a long-standing feud between a faction headed by Royal and a group of political opponents within the county administration. A story widely told and believed in West Texas, then and now, holds that several prominent Pecos County citizens met prior to the shooting and drew lots with the understanding that the man who drew the black bean would kill Royal. No one was ever brought to trial for the crime. Sheriff Royal's tombstone stands today in the old fort cemetery in Fort Stockton, Texas, with the bleak inscription *Assassinated.*

For the purposes of this book, we have adapted certain of these historical incidents. Except for the drawing of the beans and some details of the actual murder, all events described here are completely fictional.

Prologue

November 19, 1894

"He *has* to die! There's no two ways about it!"

The words rose in the still air of the judge's chambers to resonate in the iron-framed skylight set in the ceiling. Slanting across the flat roof of the Blackrock County Courthouse, cold moonlight threw a single angular shadow across the dark panes of glass.

The night was far along. The only manmade light in town streamed from the green-shaded oil lamp directly below the skylight. In its reflected glow, four men crowded around the massive oak desk where a fifth was seated. All were bundled in coats, as though they'd just come in and didn't intend to linger. From the skylight above, their faces were hidden by pulled-down hatbrims, their shapes dim and hazy through the dusty glass.

"I agree, gentlemen," the seated man said. "We have no more alternatives."

He spread his freckled hands on the desktop. His companions crowded nearer, intent on the five small objects that lay between his palms.

"That's too much!" The new speaker drew

back a step as if to leave the circle. "You're asking us to do murder. There must be another way."

The man who had spoken first barked a short laugh. "Damn right there's another way." His voice was hard, bullying. "We could all of us just kill ourselves now and save him the trouble."

For a few seconds, all of them seemed to talk at once. The skylight rang with their confusion.

". . . nothing to joke about. I'm not the lawyer here, but I'd say we're tying a noose big enough for all our necks."

". . . not murder to save your own . . ."

". . . try to buy him off. I just couldn't . . ."

". . . can count me out — and my brother, too."

"Hah! Nobody counts me out! If you're too gutless, I can . . ."

"Gentlemen!" The seated man had waited calmly while the others argued. Now his deep voice drew the circle back together. "We are bound together already by mutual culpability. I do not think prison — or being shot down in the street — preferable to the risk of hanging. Nor do I intend to live in fear of one man."

"I ain't afraid of him!"

Ignoring the interruption, the leader rose and removed his hat, revealing silvery hair.

"Five beans," he said, raking them from the desktop into the hat. "Four white, one black. I'll ask you each to draw in turn."

"Wait," one man said. "Can't we do it all together — like a firing squad?"

"I've considered that. The risks are too great. This way, only one man will know the killer." He chuckled grimly. "One *living* man," he said.

He lifted the hat toward the skylight. On the roof, the shadow drew back as the men raised their faces to look, but from the inside the panes were opaque with night. For what seemed a long time, no one moved. Then the youngest of the men stepped quickly forward.

"Hell, if nobody else has the sand, I'll go first!"

He plunged his hand into the hat. From above, it was evident he'd drawn a white bean. He cupped it for a moment, careful to hide it from the others. Then with another bark of laughter, he opened the door of the potbellied stove and flung the bean inside.

"Hah! All right, big brother, take your turn!"

His brother stared at him a moment, then reached stiffly upward, seized a white bean, glanced at it, and threw it into the fire, all in one awkward rush. The third man took his time, fingering each of the three remaining beans before he selected one. He turned away from the others, and in the moment his back was to them, palmed his white bean as smoothly as a riverboat gambler. A coin clattered into the stove.

The fourth conspirator hung back. He was older than the rest, the man who had objected in the first place. "Please," he said.

"Go on, you coward! You ain't slow when

there's money to be had."

"Please."

"I'm afraid you must," the leader said quietly. "There's no other way out for us."

"I can't."

But he advanced, raising his pale face toward the skylight. His hand trembled as he fumbled in the upraised hat. When he drew back, a single white bean remained.

"Very well." The silver-haired man took the last of the beans, studied it impassively, and threw it into the fire. His stern gaze traveled over the four other men one by one. "We are sworn, all of us. Never speak of this moment, and never reveal what bean you've drawn."

"Not likely," one of them muttered.

"This coming Sunday, we shall all be out of town, in different directions and with different destinations. Make your plans now. Our sheriff has regular habits. At midnight, he will be preparing to make his last round, seated at his desk with his back to the south window."

"My God, that's cold-blooded."

"Of course. A shotgun would be safest. When we return, each at his own pace, it will all be over. No suspicion should attach to us — so long as no one talks."

"Hah! The man who talks won't live to hang!"

"Any questions, gentlemen? Very well. I wish you good night."

Slowly, the four moved toward the door, passing out of view from the skylight. The leader remained behind to pull down the hanging lamp and tilt its shade aside. When he blew out the flame, the room was plunged into darkness except for the glow of moonlight through the unshadowed glass above.

Chapter 1

December 3, 1894

Topping a last rocky ridge, Jefferson Davis King reined in his tired mount and leaned on the saddle horn. Behind him, a saddled but riderless black gelding strained back, fighting the lead rope until King turned to quiet it with a few soft words. King's chunky roan stood motionless, sweat shiny on its flanks, stolidly ignoring the gelding. King sympathized with both animals. The ride had been long and the day hot for December, and he was as ready as his horses for a rest.

The town below promised rest, among other things. Seen from the ridge, Willow Springs was carved in relief, harsh and dusty and rugged, from the red-brown rock of the basin's floor. Homes, businesses, barns, and sheds, built of native stone or Mexican adobe, blended imperceptibly into the colors of the desert. Gleaming steel rails arrowed up from the southeast, split the town in two, then flowed away to the west and out of King's sight on their two hundred mile way to El Paso. A few riders or wagons moved along the roads into or out of town, and a buggy raised a cloud of dust in the direction of one of the outlying homesteads.

Just south of the depot and its water tower, a spreading grove of willows bordered the spring that gave the town its name and its reason for being. South again from the spring a stone courthouse squatted in the center of the town square. Even from a distance, King could pick out carved ornamentation over the tall doors, an iron fire-escape snaking past arched windows, the Texas flag flying from a staff before the door. The copper-sheathed cupola rising above the building's flat roof seemed as jarringly out of place in the dusty town as a Dresden plate on a chuck wagon's tailboard.

King studied the courthouse, guessing at where the sheriff's office might be. Almost unconsciously, he slipped a hand inside his leather jacket to touch the month-old letter that had finally caught up with him at Eagle Pass:

Jeff Davis,

I am in Need of Help & a Man I can Trust.
I have set my Hand to clean out a Nest of Villains & have contrived to make things Hot for them.
Likely matters Soon will come to Fighting. I would wish You here to watch my Back.
It has long been in my Mind to Write. I know I was Mistaken. Best we put aside our differ-

ences while there is Time. Come Soon.

C.D. Hollis
Tax Assessor & Sheriff
Blackrock County, Texas

King had heard when C.D. left the Rangers. Friends had passed along bits of gossip, news from infrequent letters. News came from Kansas, where C.D. was a peace officer, from Wyoming where he was a stock detective, from other places they were reluctant to talk about. Over a year ago, he'd brought his family back to Texas. A citizens' committee searched him out to run for sheriff in a county with some sort of trouble. He settled there, won the election, and brought in Rachel and the boys.

King had followed it all from a distance. C.D. hadn't spoken or written to him since that day in Waxahachie almost nine years ago.

"Nine years," King murmured. He'd been eighteen, a rangy, towheaded maverick of a kid convinced he was a man. Eighteen, just Rachel's age when she and C.D. married. Now King was older, more solid, his hair darkened with time, his quick blue eyes edged with crowfoot wrinkles, his hand never far from the tooled buscadero holster that rode his right hip. Nine years. A lifetime.

He remembered Rachel just as she'd been that summer before C.D. had come home, bringing his easy manner and his maturity and his stories

14

about the Ranger service. Rachel, slim and pretty in the Texas sunlight, her hair smelling of —

"No," King said aloud. *It has Long been in my Mind to Write. I know I was Mistaken.* Straightening in the saddle, King touched the roan's flanks lightly with his heels. *Best we put aside our Differences while there is Time.*

The road switchbacked down the face of the ridge, bringing King finally to the broad flat floor of the basin. Scrubby creosote bushes crowded the road. Out on the plain staghorn cholla stretched long arms toward the overcast sky. Just at the edge of town, where civilization and creation had fought to an indifferent standstill, low walls of yellow rock enclosed a barren acre. A burly brown-skinned little man perched on the top of the wall and watched King's approach with round, bright eyes.

"Thirsty?" he called hoarsely when King came within range. Lifting a flat-sided pint bottle, he shook it in the sunlight. "Come roost a spell, caw-haw."

King grinned and turned the roan. He'd noticed the stone enclosure from above, taking it for a corral or sheep pen. Now he saw he'd been wrong. A single granite monument dominated the area, surrounded by a scattering of tombstones and by many wooden crosses that stood or leaned or lay above low, stony mounds. Just inside the fence a half-dug grave waited for the little man to resume his work.

"Haw! Can't talk?" The grave digger's croak

15

was like nothing King had heard before, unless it was Captain Slater's parrot. "Seen that condition before, I have." He drew the cork, took a quick pull from the bottle, and held it out toward King. "Here's the remedy. Wet your beak and speak your name, caw-haw!"

King stepped down from the roan and took the bottle, nodding his thanks. He managed not to grimace at the raw bite of whiskey. He seldom drank and this was nothing he would've chosen on purpose, but a guest owed his host a certain amount of courtesy. With a nod, he handed back the bottle.

"Thanks. I'm Jeff King, and pleased to meet you."

"Cuervo," the little man said. He looked at King with great black eyes rimmed in white. "Crow, if you drather speak Texan. Give you two hundred dollars for that black and his silver saddle."

Wheels rattled behind King and he turned to look. A buggy was coming their way along a track that intersected the main road, drawn briskly by a high-stepping paint horse.

"Two hundred," King repeated absently. "Cash money?"

Crow coughed meditatively, "Cash or coin." He rolled himself a cigarette, twisting the ends until it looked like a Christmas candy, and accepted a match from King. "But I drather give you a bank draft. I know the money's good, and I ain't right sure about the bank, caw-haw-haw."

"You have company," King said,

Crow looked, then tucked match and cigarette into his pocket unlighted, "Oh, caw-caw-haw, that's all right. You just sit a minute and we'll finish our talk, you and me."

The rig was close enough now for the driver to see and perhaps resent his stare. King watched her anyway. She handled the paint with the light touch of a charioteer, slender and assured on the black leather seat. Her hair, left free to blow with the wind, was as black as her eyes and her tailored riding dress. Her face reminded King of a statue he'd seen pictured in a magazine, the face of a goddess in pale and perfect marble,

The girl — woman, King amended; she didn't look older than twenty, but there was nothing girlish about her — drew her buggy to a smooth stop alongside King's horses. She looked down at him for a moment, her black eyes cool and level and too deep to see into. Then she smiled at Crow.

"Good morning, Cuervo. Maria is well."

Her voice reminded King of the silver altar bell he'd heard in a Mexican cathedral. He took off his hat.

"*Gracias*, Miss Diana," Crow said. "Good of you to come by," The speech sent Crow off into another coughing fit. When it passed, he bobbed his head toward King. "Might as well meet Jeff King. Just now blew in with the wind, he did, caw."

Diana. King fitted the name to her at once.

17

"Your servant, miss," he said.

"Mr. King," the bell chimed. Its note was faintly inquisitive. She looked at the saddled gelding. "Are you riding in company?"

King started to speak, then shook his head. Something — the whiskey, most likely — had filled his throat with sand.

"Has a mite of trouble talking, he does," Crow put in helpfully. "That be an extra horse he's trailing. I'm offering to buy him."

"I see. Is that your trade, Mr. King, selling horses?"

King swallowed and tried his voice again. "No, ma'am. The black isn't mine."

"Then you're a horse thief?"

Crow went into a whooping fit of coughing or laughter. King felt his face burn.

"No," he said again, mentally cursing himself. It wasn't like him to get this flustered over a pretty face. "But he isn't mine to sell. He's meant for someone else."

"Oh?" A ripple of curiosity rose in her black eyes. She let the word hang as a question for a moment, then smiled at him. "Will you be staying long in Willow Springs?"

"A few days, I expect. As long as my business takes."

"Maybe I'll see you again, then." To Crow, she said, "I'll be back tomorrow. Don't let Maria worry about anything."

Crow ducked his head. "You bet, missy, and we thanks you kindly. Give my best to your ma and pa. You tell them Cuervo sends his best, caw-caw-haw."

"I will. Good morning, Mr. King."

She shook the reins and the paint responded instantly, wheeling the light buggy around. She had time for a bright, impersonal smile at King, and then the rig was flying down the road toward town. King stood watching.

"Pretty thing, ain't she?" Crow said. "Caw-haw, now about that gelding. Being as you don't claim him, who do I see about his price?"

Bringing himself back from his thoughts, King grinned. "Sorry. The gelding's a present, not for sale."

He hesitated, wanting to know more about Diana but unwilling to ask. It didn't matter, he reasoned. C.D. would laugh at him, but could surely tell him all about her. He looked at the pile of dirt from the grave, reddish cloddy clay heavily marbled with broken white rock. A pick lay across the mound.

"Must be slow work, digging here."

Crow retrieved the cigarette and lighted it, gusting out a cloud of bitter gray smoke. He coughed, then used his sleeve to wipe first his eyes and then the neck of the whiskey bottle.

"Go again? Well, I'll just have another, then. Everything's slow hereabouts, caw-caw-cawf, birthing and dying and mail and grave digging. Easy digging, though. Been used before."

With surprising agility, he hopped off the wall and bent to scratch at his mound. In a moment, he brought up a crumbling shank of white bone.

"Here go." He laughed at King's hesitation. " 'Twon't bite you now, if'n it would have once." He cocked his head to one side, squinting at the relic. "Apache, that one is. Fought it out here with a company of Rangers, back before the War, likely before you were borned. Them as died is buried here, horses and Apaches and Rangers together."

King reached to take the bone, interested. "Rangers, too?" He turned it in his hands. "How can you tell which were which?"

"Rangers planted their own deeper. Like the Mexican folk says: 'Bury a Ranger deep. A shorter *jornada* for the devil.' "

His face gone cold, King studied the smaller man. Crow gazed back with round, unblinking eyes. After a moment, King shook his head slightly. "Grave digging your regular work, is it?" he asked.

"Grave digger's what I am." Crow finished the cigarette with a second enormous puff, lived through another bout of coughing, and tossed the smoking twist of paper into the grave. "That and keep the courthouse clean, judge's chambers and sheriff's office. And the top of the bar in the Lost Mule Tavern."

"I guess you'd know the sheriff pretty well?"

"Knowed quite a few. Been nigh a dozen since the county started. Some's as moved on, some's left the office." He made a quick peck of a nod. "Some's stops right here."

"You want to talk to the sheriff about buying the gelding, then. It's meant for him." He watched for a reaction, but Crow only blinked at him solemnly. "I wonder if you'd know where I might find him this time of day."

"Depends," Crow said. "Depends which one you want. Him they call sheriff struts around in daylight. Him that was sheriff sleeps deep in the dark."

He cocked his head toward the mound with the granite marker, but his gaze stayed on King.

"Buried deep," he said.

Chapter 2

November 19, 1894

In the dark hallway of the courthouse, the five men split up. Henry Drumm went first, striding briskly along the hallway toward open air and freedom. He hesitated a moment at the cross-corridor, then chose the south steps. The sheriff's office was beside that entrance, its doorway opening into the hall and its window looking out on the midnight square. Probably Sheriff Hollis was out on a late-night round, but he might be in the office. Henry Drumm was a gambler, and he weighed the risk with quiet enjoyment.

Ever since he'd come to Willow Springs, he'd been riding a winning streak. A few errands for the judge, a message sent here and there, and he was within reach of as much money as even his gambler's heart craved — all safe and legal. No document anywhere implicated him. Now even taking care of Hollis was out of his hands. Somebody else would have that little pleasure, and Drumm's hands would be clean.

Chuckling into his beard, he paused to finger the hard shape of the white bean he'd palmed. Then he tucked it carefully away in his watch pocket, strode past the locked door of the sheriff's office, and went out into the night.

Cy Timm scurried along the west hall and tiptoed down the stairs ahead of the Parnell brothers. Before he reached the outer door, he heard their steps and the mutter of their voices behind him. Frantically, he darted into the dark recess behind the stairs. He couldn't face anyone else just then. He needed to be alone to think.

Heavy steps rang on the treads above him. Dust filtered down on his bowed shoulders. Timm held his breath, wrinkling his nose to stifle a sneeze. The sound of voices covered the small wheeze of his breathing. The Parnells were quarreling again.

". . . planning?" Eli was saying. Timm strained to hear, then jumped as Buck's answer came almost against his ear.

"Planning. Remember about the black bean?"

"Hush!" Eli's voice sank to a whisper so Timm could hear only snatches. ". . . better than . . . jokes . . . weren't the one."

"Somebody had to be the one. You didn't draw it."

Hinges creaked and the sounds moved away from Timm to be sliced off completely by the closing of the heavy door. Tim crept from his hole and peered through the glass panes. The Parnells were just outside, speaking more softly now. Finally, they said their good-nights and parted.

Eli moved out of sight, but Buck paused a few paces away to light a cigar. Watching him, Timm tried to put together what he'd heard. Buck had hinted to Eli that he'd drawn the black bean, but Timm knew better. He shuddered, remembering the sight of it, black as death, resting in his own palm. He still couldn't bear to think what that meant, so he turned with relief to this new puzzle. Had two of the beans been black, then?

For a moment, he considered the idea. The judge might have planned it that way. Judge Blankenship was a clever man; he'd been the one to think out the plan that was making them all rich. Maybe he'd had some reason to slip a second black bean into the hat.

No. Timm remembered staring at the beans beforehand. Four had been alabaster white, the fifth black as — as death. Buck had lied to his brother. As he quietly eased the heavy door open, Cy Timm wondered why.

Chapter 3

December 3, 1894

Jeff King rode slowly into Willow Springs, the gelding snubbed up hard on his left. A short Winchester carbine lay across his left arm. Avoiding the courthouse and the town square, he angled off onto one of the random rutted paths that passed for streets. At the third house along the way he halted and tied off his horses to the cornerpost of the rickety picket fence.

The house, like the town itself, seemed shabby and rundown, but King saw beyond its appearance. The crumbling adobe walls, drab and needing a new coat of plaster, would hold warmth inside in winter and keep the heat out in summer. Set high in the walls, the narrow windows protected against dust and prying eyes. The shady porch had begun to rot where rainwater had seeped through a neglected roof, but a stack of new flooring waited like a promise beside the front door.

A brown and white dog lay under the porch, his head lifted. Making his judgment, the dog rose, stretched, and trotted over to sniff at the visitor. Still holding the carbine, King knelt to scratch the brindled ears. Most often, C.D. had told him once, a friendly dog meant friendly people.

"Good boy."

He drew a strip of venison jerky from his shirt pocket, broke it in two, held out the pieces. The dog scooped them up eagerly with his warm tongue and whined for more.

Under King's exploring hand, ribs stood out gaunt beneath the tangled coat.

"Nobody looking after you, boy? Why's that?"

He rose and stepped up onto the porch, the dog trotting anxiously at his side. Only a tattered screen door blocked the entrance. Above it a polished wooden plaque carried a single word: Hollis. King rapped sharply on the facing, waited, then pushed inside.

The house was empty, smelling of dust and abandonment. Standing the carbine beside the door, King moved from room to room. Most of the furniture remained, but the personal items that gave a house life were gone. The house was dead, as dead as its owner. Whatever had become of Rachel and the children, they no longer lived there.

King came back into the parlor. A heavy horsehair sofa, its wooden arms and framing richly carved with fruit, stood worn and dusty against the near wall. A matching chair filled one corner and a tiny Spanish-style fireplace another. Across from the doorway two unused packing cases lay side by side on the flowered carpet.

The house in Waxahachie always smelled of baking and fresh-cut roses and the warm leather of his father's books and black medical bag. The parlor carpet was purple with a golden fringe and tiny flowers scattered through the pattern. The boy liked to stretch out in front of the broad hearth, his dog beside him. He watched while his parents played Chinese checkers or his father read aloud from the big Bible he knew almost by heart.

Then the smell was of sickness. Neighbors and ladies from the church served food and talked quietly in the kitchen. At the cool end of the parlor, two coffins lay across the seats of kitchen chairs. C.D. stood beside them, lean and wiry at eighteen, just twice as old as King.

"It'll be all right, Jeff Davis. I'll look after you and Nancy."

Nancy was six, all big eyes and golden hair and trembling mouth. She didn't know enough to cry, or to worry about the Orphans' Home. King did.

"You won't. You never liked Pa. You're never here."

"I'll be here now. For as long as you all need me."

"You won't. Why should you? You're only half my brother!"

The dog whined. King came back to the empty room, aware of a dull ache in his left hand. He looked down, watching his clenched fist pound time after time into the adobe wall beside the doorframe. After a moment, he willed it to stop.

The crumbling white plaster was smeared with blood.

"All right," King said softly. "We'll see."

He picked up the carbine and strode quickly out to his horses. Slipping the carbine into its boot, he drew a longbarreled rifle from a boot on the opposite side of the saddle. He levered a shell into the chamber and lowered the hammer to half-cock. The guns were a set, Model '86 Winchesters of the same caliber and matching serial numbers. He didn't expect trouble yet, but before he was through in Willow Springs, he knew he'd need them. He meant to be ready.

Returning the rifle to its place, he mounted and rode back toward the courthouse. The brown and white dog barked once, then trotted expectantly along behind.

Up close, the town square confirmed King's earlier judgment. If there was anything fancy or frivolous in Willow Springs, the businesses didn't show it. The single livery stable, set back toward the depot, looked spare and clean, meant for men who depended on their animals. The wagons King saw were solid utility rigs, and the saddle horses wore roping saddles with little ornament. Around the town square, it was the same. Roughly painted signs identified a hardware store, a meat market, a general mercantile, and two saloons. Neither storekeepers nor shoppers moved on the packed-earth walks.

King marked all the signs of a town with little

money to spare, then looked thoughtfully at the massive stone courthouse. In the shade of a lone tree near its door stood Miss Diana's black runabout, the paint horse dozing between the shafts. On the other side of the wide front door was an iron hitching post below a sign reading *Sheriff*.

For the first time since his talk with Crow, King quirked his mouth into a smile. He guided the roan over and tied both horses to the post. Then he slipped the carbine from its boot and walked across to E. Parnell and Son, Hardware Merchants.

"Say, mister —"

The man who met him in the doorway was square and sturdy — oak sheathed and copper riveted, King thought, a live advertisement for his hardware. Once, he might have looked like a new Concord coach, tight-sprung and varnished to a shine with his red hair slicked back like the final coat of paint. Hard wear in the desert had seasoned him, though, drawing out all the oil and leaving him faded and brittle-looking as an old buckboard.

"Linseed oil," King said.

The storekeeper — E. Parnell, King supposed — blinked. "Well, yes, I have some." His voice crackled like dry grass in the wind. "But what I meant to say —"

He stopped, looking at the dog that still tagged at King's heels. King stepped past him into the relative darkness of the store's interior.

"What I really need is some ammunition. Two

29

boxes of .45-90 smokeless with the heaviest loads you have."

"Two boxes," Parnell echoed automatically. He looked at the dog again, then at King. "Isn't that — ?" He stopped, then said, "I don't carry .45-90s. Most folks think they kick too much. And there's nothing around here big enough to hunt with them."

"We'll see," King said. "How about .45-70s, then?"

"That dog." Parnell hesitated, glancing across the street. "Listen, being a stranger here, you probably didn't notice about the hitch rail there." He pointed an axehandle arm. "It's for the sheriff's use, see. I'll just —"

"No matter," King interrupted. "I've got business with the sheriff. How about that ammunition?"

"But —"

"Does my dog bother you? I can put him outside."

King knelt to catch the animal's collar, still watching Parnell. He didn't know what had spooked the storekeeper, and he was interested. *"A man who runs scared generally has a reason,"* C.D. had said once. *"A good lawman, he'll wonder what the reason is."*

"Looks like he's adopted me," he said. "You wouldn't know his name, would you?"

Automatically, Parnell began, "Hollis called —" He cut himself off. "No, no — I don't know him."

"Well, I'll call him Holley," King said easily. "That's the nickname of a friend of mine. That all right with you, Holley?" He rubbed the dog's head, then looked up at Parnell. "By the way, I wonder if you'd know where I might find Rachel Hollis?"

"I — she —" Under its coat of varnish, Parnell's face had paled. "Listen, mister, who — ?"

He broke off abruptly, relief and apprehension mingled in his face. A bandy-legged young man in a tall black hat came out of the main door of the courthouse. A badge glinted silver on his vest. He turned as though speaking to someone behind him, then noticed King's horses and came down the steps with the swift, confident strut of a fighting cock.

"Is that a feather in his hatband?" King asked, rising. "My Lord, I believe it is. You all put on quite a show here."

"What?" Parnell shook himself. "That's the sheriff. And there's Judge Blankenship, just come out of the restaurant. I'll just step across —"

Without finishing, he hurried woodenly into the street. King stepped out onto the porch to watch. The man he took for Judge Blankenship was tall with a lean, patrician face and a mane of silver hair. King guessed him five years either way from fifty. An older man scurried like a plump mouse at his elbow. The two of them started across the street toward the courthouse, then saw the sheriff and paused. King waited for

31

another person to emerge from the courthouse, but the bronze-sheathed doors swung closed.

Without a glance at Parnell or the others, the sheriff reached the hitching post, untied King's horses, and waved his hat at the roan. Holley gave an angry yelp and dashed out of the store, barking furiously. The horses shied off down the street with Parnell in stiff-legged pursuit.

Still barking, Holley circled the sheriff. Startled, the man turned and aimed a kick at the dog. Then, abruptly, he clapped his hat back on his head and dropped his hand to the holster at his left hip.

King whistled piercingly. "Holley! Here, boy!"

Still snarling, the dog dropped back. The sheriff raised his eyes to look at King, then aimed his rooster-strut toward the hardware store. He was younger than King, not more than twenty-three, with the same square build and red hair as Eli Parnell. His varnish hadn't faded yet, and he wore it with an air of cocky assurance.

"I hope you're rich or lucky, Deputy," King greeted him. "I think pretty highly of my livestock — the dog especially."

"Fact is, I'm both, friend," the sheriff said.

He stopped short of the porch and looked up at King. Quick blue eyes frowned at the carbine, the short vaquero jacket, the long revolver angled butt-forward in its holster. Finally his gaze came back to King's face, studying him as a woodsman studies a tree to be felled.

"Rich and lucky both," he said. "Handsome,

too." With two quick strides, he circled King's flank and stepped onto the porch. He still had to look up at King. He hooked his thumbs into his belt, his left hand an inch from the butt of the nickel-plated six-gun. "Suppose you tell me your name and what you want here — and what you're doing with that mutt?"

"The dog's mine. My name's King. My business is with Sheriff Hollis."

"There ain't no Sheriff Hollis, friend. I'm Sheriff Buck Parnell, and I'm asking your business."

"None too politely, either. I never figured C.D. would turn his office over to a hotheaded kid."

A little way down the street, the older Parnell was struggling with the two horses. King saw with interest that Diana was helping. The black was still spooked, and she was holding its bit while she spoke to it. King wasn't sure where she'd come from, but she hadn't been in sight earlier. The judge and his companion had come up from the other direction and now stood listening to King and Buck Parnell.

"Listen, friend," Parnell said. "This is about as polite as I get. In another minute, I'm going to take that carbine away from you and slap you in a cell until you're ready to be civil."

"Are you?" King asked softly. He hooked his thumb over the Winchester's hammer, ready to cock it. He'd come in looking for trouble, and he was pleased he'd found it so easily. "I don't think so."

The sheriff squared around. He looked uncertain which way his tree might fall, but King saw no trace of fear in his eyes.

"Last chance, friend," he said.

"Just a moment, Buck. I believe we have a misunderstanding here."

Judge Blankenship's voice was deep and impressive. Buck hesitated, but didn't look away from King.

"My business, Judge," he said.

"County business," Blankenship contradicted pleasantly. He stepped forward, placing a fatherly hand on Buck's shoulder and giving King a guarded smile. "Homer Blankenship, sir. Do I understand you to be seeking C.D. Hollis?"

"I'm Jeff King. And I am looking for C.D. right enough."

"I regret to say that mortality has preceded you. I've appointed Sheriff Buck Parnell to fill the office until conditions permit an election. Buck and his brother, Eli, whom you've already met, are two of our leading citizens."

"Brother?" King let his curiosity take him off the main trail. "Seems like it should be E. Parnell and *Sons*, then."

Blankenship smiled again. "The store was started by these boys' father, Mr. Eli Parnell, Senior. The reason the name was not changed after his death —"

"— is none of his damn business!" Buck cut in. He pushed against Blankenship's restraining hand, fresh anger on his face.

"You must not have much business of your own, friend, to take so much interest in ours."

"Just a habit."

"Well, it's a bad one. What the judge is telling you with his fancy talk is that Hollis is dead. Deader'n Moses, and good riddance. That satisfy you?"

"No."

Eli Parnell had come near enough to listen. Diana was hanging back. The commotion had brought a few people out of the stores and saloons. Blankenship glanced around.

"Perhaps we could talk more freely —" he began. King interrupted him.

"Who killed him?"

The judge's eyes narrowed. "No one said he was killed."

"Listen, Judge, he knows," Buck said. "He come in here with that dog. Claims it's his."

"That's right. And I'm still asking who killed his last owner."

For a minute, no one spoke. Surprisingly, it was Eli Parnell who broke the silence.

"Nobody knows who. He was shot. About three weeks ago. In his office. With a shotgun. In the back."

"Not in the back," the mousy little man said quickly. King looked at him and he edged back a step. "I mean — it wasn't. Not in the back."

"That's all right, Cy," Blankenship said. "Cy Timm, Mr. King, our county clerk. He's quite right. Sheriff Hollis was facing his assailant." His thin lips tightened in remembered distaste. "The nature of his wound left no doubt of that."

"That still makes it murder, doesn't it?"

The dozen or so watchers let out a murmur. They had edged closer during the conversation. Blankenship looked around in annoyance.

"I was about to suggest we discuss this inside. If you'll step across to the courthouse, Sheriff Parnell will give you all the particulars — assuming you have some legitimate interest in the matter."

King figured he had enough listeners so his words would spread all over town. He raised his voice.

"Yes, I do have an interest. I intend to find his killer." He looked around at the crowd, then came back to Buck and the judge. "You can save me a lot of time. Just which one of you good people shot C.D.?"

Chapter 4

November 19, 1894

Judge Homer Blankenship walked briskly along the hall until the deep shadows hid him from the others. Then he stopped, waiting for the sounds of their departure to die away. Satisfied, he unlocked a paneled door and felt his way down a narrow spiral stair. At the bottom, he emerged into the courtroom like a king entering his palace.

Solemnly, he paced across the broad floor to the judge's bench, where he scratched a match into life and lit a pair of tall candles. Subdued in the faint light, the flags of Texas and the United States flanked the bench. The jury box was a featureless black shadow, and the cavernous darkness outside the candles' reach held the pews where the unelect sat to plead their causes or watch the workings of the court.

Sliding into his seat, Blankenship smiled. Soon he would preside over the inquest into the death of C.D. Hollis. After that, if fortune favored him, he would try the most famous murder case in Texas history. He would be famous, a fit candidate for a higher court or even for the governor's office. Given Hollis's corpse, all he would need was a defendant.

He had a couple of candidates in mind.

Allowing the others their haste, Eli and Buck Parnell walked along the western hallway to the stairs.

"I need your help at the store," Eli said.

Buck laughed. "After what we just did, you're going off to count nails?" he asked. "Big brother, you do beat hell."

"A shipment of hand tools came on the afternoon train. They have to be uncrated and checked against the manifest."

"That's a good two hours' work. It's past midnight now."

"Then they'll have to be priced and put on the shelves."

"Not by me. Not tonight."

"You're a full partner," Eli said reproachfully. "That store's our livelihood. I'd think you'd want to do your part."

"Not tonight, Eli. I've got things to do."

They came to the stairwell and started down. Eli held stiffly to the rail and squinted at the dim shape of the steps as he descended.

"What do you have to do that's more important than making our living?" He put an awkward hand on Buck's shoulder. "I hope you're not gambling again."

Buck shook him off. "Nobody's business if I was," he snapped. "The money's mine."

"It comes from the store."

"Some of it. It makes up for me not getting my rights from Pa's estate. You took care of that, big brother."

"That money went into the store."

"So you say. I don't recall being asked."

They had come to the first floor landing. Eli reached out and caught Buck's arm again. Again Buck tried to shake free, but this time the strong fingers held him like a wooden vise.

"I asked where you were going," Eli said. "I'll have an answer."

"You ain't my pa," Buck snarled. "No matter what you think!" He wrenched away, rubbing his bruised arm. "Could be I got some planning to do. Think on that."

"Planning?"

"Planning. Remember about the black bean?"

"Hush!" Eli peered anxiously around the dark hall. "You know better than to speak of that. Don't make jokes! You weren't the one."

"Somebody has to be. You didn't get it, did you?"

"Just hush!"

Eli pushed open the door, looked around carefully, then held it for Buck. Outside, the night was clear, the moonlight bright enough to dim the stars. A chill wind whispered out of the desert. Eli pulled his coat closer about him.

"I'm sorry," he said very softly. "I never thought you'd be the one."

Buck shrugged. "Who better? You never think

about anything except that damn store." He drew a cigar from his coat pocket and offered one to Eli. "Quit looking behind every bush, now. It's all right for us to be together. We're brothers."

"Even so, we'd best go different ways," Eli murmured. "We'll talk tomorrow." More loudly, he added, "Good night, then. I'll be at the store if you want me."

"All right."

"Are you going by the house?"

"If you want me to."

"I wish you would. Tell Sheila I'll be working late."

"I'll tell her. Good night — brother!"

Chapter 5

December 3, 1894

"Do I need to ask again? I want the one that killed C.D."

As if the question were a noose, it jerked Cy Timm up on his toes in an involuntary twitch. He let out a startled squeak and stared at King. Eli Parnell stood expressionless as a fencepost. Buck's face turned a shade grimmer and he wrapped his fingers around the butt of his nickel-plated Colt. The others who formed his little audience reacted with surprise or silence, anger or laughter, each according to his nature. Amid their noise, King heard an indignant stroke of Diana's silver bell. He wanted to look at her but kept his attention on Buck, waiting to see if the new sheriff would draw.

"Listen, friend —"

"The ancient Greeks," Judge Blankenship cut in firmly, "held hospitality as a solemn duty. 'Welcome the coming, speed the departing, guest.' You, Mr. King, come as a guest in our fair town."

Blankenship's smooth face was untroubled, though no trace of civility remained in his icy tone. He took another step, intentionally inter-posing himself between King and Buck Par-nell.

"But hospitality depends on the conduct of the guest. You have abused ours." He swept his arm in an oratorical gesture, taking in the whole town. "We here are honest citizens of Willow Springs. I think we have the right to resent your insult."

"No insult intended," King said. "A man's been murdered, a lawman. Most likely somebody in Willow Springs killed him. Seems to me your new sheriff ought to have that somebody in jail by now — unless he's been too busy welcoming guests to your fair town."

"You underrate the problem, sir," Blankenship said calmly. "The late Sheriff Hollis had many enemies. Since you apparently were his friend, I'll spare you the details of his conduct. But there are many who had reason to kill him, if only to rid the town of a menace."

"Damn right," Buck put in. "Myself, I think it was a stranger, somebody Hollis did wrong back in Kansas, maybe. Probably I'll never find out for sure."

King felt fresh anger climbing his backbone, but he kept his voice soft. He'd done what he set out to do; by dark, everyone for miles would know he was after the killer. An open fight wouldn't gain him anything now.

"Probably you won't," he told Buck. "But I just expect you've been working yourself to death trying." He lifted the carbine and rested its barrel against his shoulder. "Maybe I'll stay around and help you look."

"I don't want any help."

"Didn't ask if you did. I just think I'd like to be around when you pin the medal on him." He looked at the shiny badge on Buck's vest. "Unless somebody's already done that."

Buck's face flushed a deeper red. For a second, King thought he'd gone too far. Then Blankenship spoke again.

"That's enough, King. We've endured you this long, but hospitality has its limits. You're not staying here. If you aren't out of Willow Springs by —"

Eli Parnell moved. His wooden face looked past the group around King, toward three riders coming up the road from the south. He placed his hand on Blankenship's arm, stopping the judge in midsentence.

"Bold as brass," Eli said.

Blankenship turned to look, then glanced back at King with a speculative frown. Buck Parnell grinned.

The three newcomers reined back their horses near the depot, separated from the townspeople by the double steel bands of the railroad track. For the moment they sat motionless, studying the gathering in front of Parnell's store. Puzzled, King studied them in turn.

Two of the men were Mexican. Both wore sombreros and tight leather jackets much like King's. The younger looked a year or so shy of twenty, with a thin, high-cheekboned face that showed only a wisp of mustache. The man on the other flank, face lined and ageless as fine leather, thick mustache heavily laced with silver, might have been the other's father. Both were armed with rifle and revolver. The younger man carried two pistols, one in a hip holster and the other thrust into the sash at his waist.

The third rider was unarmed. He was a gray, spare man mounted on a tall gray horse. He gazed at King and the others with faded gray eyes in a thin hawk face.

"Your lucky day, friend," Buck said. "You're hell bent on finding somebody with a good reason to kill Hollis, and there sits the man with the best reason in town." He nodded toward the man on the gray horse. "Suppose you just go over —"

"Buck Parnell! You know better than that." Still holding the reins of King's horses, Diana strode to the porch, leading the animals with her. Her voice rang now with steel instead of silver. "My father had reason to hate Hollis — same as I did. But he would have faced him in front of the whole town and shot him down, not sneaked up on him in the dark like a coward or a woman!"

Buck took a step back, caught by surprise by her fury. "Now, Diana, I never said he did it." He gestured toward King. "It's this drifter. He's the one making trouble."

The man on the gray horse leaned in the saddle and spoke to the younger vaquero. Immediately, the young man pushed his horse forward, parting

the crowd until he came even with Diana. Bending toward her, he murmured his message.

Black hair flashed as she shook her head. She
turned on King. "Maybe you'd like to take it up
with *me*," she challenged.

"No, ma'am," King said, "Not just yet."

The vaucro's face was flushed with injured
pride. He reached out toward Diana's shoulder,
then thought better of it and drew back. Sitting
his horse in stiff anger, he glared at King. His
older companion dismounted and walked
through the muttering crowd to stop before
Diana. Whatever he said carried more weight.
She lashed King's horses with their own reins,
sending them whirling white-eyed away from her.
Turning without another glance at the group on
the porch, she strode rapidly toward the man
who had sent for her. The vaqueros followed
more slowly, the younger one backing his horse
to keep King and the others in sight. Buck
Parnell laughed.

"Take your pick, friend," he said. "If you tan-
gle with Diana, best watch for teeth and claws.
If you'd rather go up against her old man and
his army —"

"He have a name?" King interrupted. He wondered if it was a rule that whatever Buck laughed
at wouldn't strike him funny at all.

"— why maybe you can call in the Rangers for
help. Name? Hell, you know so much, I figured
you knew him."

"Castleberry," Judge Blankenship supplied

softly. He still regarded King with a faintly quizzical expression.

"Dallas Castleberry?" King hid his surprise beneath another look at the gray-eyed rider. Half of Texas knew the name. Few knew the man.

"That's right," Eli said, his voice dry and hard. "Damn his soul."

King looked at him for a moment with new interest. Then he turned his attention back to the little group by the depot. Castleberry was speaking to Diana, saying something she evidently didn't want to hear. Abruptly, she tossed her head and walked back toward her buggy.

"I figured you'd know him already," Buck laughed. He seemed to be enjoying himself. "You being a friend of Hollis and all, and him and Castleberry being so tight until —"

"How about Miss Diana?" King interrupted, and cursed himself. His anger was getting the better of everything he'd learned — everything C.D. had tried to teach him.

"A man wants to tell you something, let him, Jeff Davis. You just look interested and keep quiet, he'll tell you things you couldn't beat out of him with a stick."

Well, whatever Buck had been about to tell him was gone. He watched Diana reach the buggy, put her hand under the seat, and draw out a small-bore carbine.

"What about her?" he repeated. "Since the two of you seem to be so tight."

Buck's eyes flicked toward the courthouse and

his self-assurance wavered for a second. Then he laughed again. "Hell, friend, you don't know much," he said. "Castleberry's daughter, and just as stiff-necked as her old man." He frowned in sudden suspicion. "Hey, were you *really* a friend of Hollis, or are you just shooting us a line?"

"Could be," King said. He stepped down from the porch and walked toward Castleberry and his men. The brown and white dog loped along for a few steps, then swung off to trot over to Diana.

"Traitor," King muttered, and then all his attention was centered on the rancher and his outriders.

"Never give a man the jump on you." C.D.'s voice again, inside his head but clear as it had been in life. King couldn't remember how long ago that must have been — fifteen, sixteen years ago, maybe, when C.D. was newly in the Rangers and King was still just a kid — but he remembered the words. *"Start out on top and stay there. Run him or he'll run you."*

The three men, all mounted again, had spread in a shallow crescent to meet him. From the corner of his eye, he saw Diana cock the carbine and take station on his flank. There were holes in his education, he realized. C.D. had never told him how to stop a woman from getting the jump on him. And the situation had never come up before.

As if the railroad tracks marked some kind of border, Dallas Castleberry started forward as soon as King crossed them. King stopped, resting the carbine's barrel against his shoulder, and waited for him.

The gray took its own pace, and Castleberry seemed as much a part of its motion as the limb of a breeze-blown tree. He watched King like a hawk sizing up a mouse while his vaqueros scanned every window or doorway or rooftop around the square. The three had nearly reached King when the gray horse stopped without any apparent command. Castleberry looked down from the saddle, gray eyes bleak.

"You've signed on with the wrong outfit." The rancher's voice blew on King like a prairie norther, cold and gritty. "Two ways you can go. The easy one's to get up on your silver saddle and ride out."

King held his face expressionless. He didn't like looking up at Castleberry. He didn't like Castleberry's men on his flanks, or Diana behind him somewhere with her little rifle.

Run him or he'll run you. "Or?" he asked.

Castleberry inclined his head. "Or you can face off with Saul and Octavio. Now or later."

"Pass," King said. "For now. I mean to talk to you, but I don't know there's any quarrel between us — unless you have to have it that way."

Castleberry raised an eyebrow. "You *mean* to talk to me, do you?" This time, King saw the rancher's knees tighten. The gray horse took a dancing step, edging into King and forcing him back. "Best you understand I set the terms here."

King didn't move the Winchester, but he thumbed back the hammer with a click all three men heard.

"I'll talk, but I won't be pushed," he said. "Best you understand that. Two ways you can go. Easy one's to stand your mount back a little."

The older vaquero was off to King's right now, and the body of the gray horse blocked the younger one from his sight. He wasn't sure where Diana was, but he'd worry about her last. He'd never had to face the prospect of shooting a woman, and that way he probably wouldn't have to worry about it. He shifted his weight carefully, watching for a sign from Castleberry. If the sign was wrong, he'd need a lot of luck, more than he was likely to get.

Castleberry studied him a moment longer, eyes prying like fingers for a sign of weakness. Then the rancher snorted and tossed his head like a stallion — Diana's gesture, King remembered. The gray pranced back a step and stopped.

"All right. Speak your piece."

"I'm here for the man who killed C.D. Hollis. I mean to have him, whoever he happens to be. Those nice folks over by the hardware said I should talk to you."

"Did they?" Castleberry glanced that way. For a moment, his lips quirked in a near-smile. "Don't give up easy, I'll give them that." He frowned at King. "Have I mistook you?"

The older vaquero pushed his horse a little

49

closer and spoke to Castleberry in Spanish. King caught the word *Ranger*.

"The hell you say?" Castleberry murmured. He looked over King's gunbelt and rigging. Then, in spite of his age, he stepped down from the gray as nimbly as a cat coming off a fence. "Have I mistook you?" he repeated.

"Depends. You've guessed I don't like looking up to a man. What else do you think?"

The rancher jerked a quick nod toward Blankenship and the Parnell brothers, still watching from the porch. "I thought you worked for the judge's gang — thought they'd hired a new man-killer, since their first one didn't pan out." His eyes searched King's face. "I've been figuring a Ranger might come, right enough. Are you the one they sent?"

King didn't answer right away. "Nobody sent me," he said finally. "I came to see Sheriff Hollis."

"Friend of yours, was he?"

"I was bringing him that horse with the Mexican saddle." He felt his throat tighten for a second. "It'll belong to his boys, now, when I find them." He looked at Castleberry. "I mean to find his killer first."

The rancher's expression changed, though King couldn't have said how. It was like a cloud's shadow sliding along the face of a cliff.

"That black's no horse for young'uns," Castleberry said. He thought for a moment, his eyes distant. "Ride over to my place in the morning.

Bring the black. We'll work something out."

"I told you my intentions, I mean to hear what you have to say about C.D."

"Not here."

"Inside, then. You pick the place."

Castleberry shook his head. "Not in this town. I won't set foot across those tracks. I won't talk here. I won't do business here. When the spur line to my ranch is finished, I won't even have to order supplies here, nor pick up shipments. Before I'm done, I'll see it wiped off God's earth."

He turned away abruptly, leading the gray toward the hitching rail in front of the depot. The vaqueros sat motionless facing King, a rear guard waiting for orders.

"Where do I find your place?" King asked.

Castleberry didn't look back. "Far as I'm concerned, you're standing on it. Headquarters is south."

King considered for a moment, then went to recover his horses. Diana Castleberry was striding back toward her buggy. She slid the little rifle under its seat. Then, perhaps sensing King's eyes on her, she turned and gave him a cold, deliberate stare. Swinging up to the buggy's seat, she snapped the reins. The paint horse wheeled the light rig around.

King watched the buggy bump across the railroad tracks and raise a feather of dust along the long, straight road that ran south. He wasn't sure, but he thought Diana turned to look back just as the road carried her out of sight behind a rise of ground.

Any woman was a mystery, King mused, but Diana was a question for Solomon. She had been friendly, then angry, then ready to kill him, all on account of C.D. What had Buck said? *"Best watch for teeth and claws."* King could believe that. And if the Castleberry outfit didn't trade in Willow Springs, why had she been north of town so early?

She was a mystery, and a dangerous one. King didn't like the thought of facing her and her carbine again. As he walked slowly back toward the square, it occurred to him that C.D. Hollis had taught him a lot, but almost none of it pertained to women. He'd have to rely on his own judgment there.

King left his horses at the livery for a feed and rest. Leaving Holley contentedly panting in the doorway, he slung saddlebags across his left shoulder, rested the carbine on his right and sauntered back along the square. Buck and the judge were nowhere in sight, but he saw Eli Parnell watching impassively through his store window. Beside the doorway of the Lost Mule Saloon, Crow leaned on a broom as if it were a prophet's staff. He stared with interest but no hint of recognition as King passed. A moment later, Cy Timm emerged from the barber shop at the northeast corner of the square. Catching sight of King, he gave a startled squeak and scurried back inside. King grinned. If nothing else, he'd provoked plenty of interest in his presence.

He went into Higginbotham's Grocery, leaned his carbine against the counter, and waited for a man in a bloodstained white apron to finish sweeping a week's worth of dirty sawdust out the back door.

"I'll need a few things," he said.

"I've got a few." The man was sixty, squat, almost bald. He worked a shovel around in a barrel in the corner and pulled it out heaping with fresh sawdust. "Be with you in a minute. You can start counting them things off. I'll remember."

"Slab of bacon. Loaf of bread, if it's fresh."

"Baked this morning." The older man scattered another shovel of sawdust behind the counter and squinted at the effect. "What else?"

"Good-size steak and some stew meat."

"You're a hungry man with a dog, are you?"

"That's right."

"Brown and white dog."

King nodded. The grocer put away his shovel.

"Eggs is good for a dog that hasn't been fed in awhile. Shines up his coat and fills in between his ribs." He thrust out a strong red hand to King. "I'm Higginbotham. Which party are you working for?"

"Neither," King said. He gave his name with complete confidence that Higginbotham already knew it. "You keep ammunition?"

The butcher held his grip while he sized King

up the way he might have examined a side of beef. "If Eli wouldn't sell you none, he figures you're hired to Castleberry. No other reason for that old wooden Indian to pass by a dime."

"I haven't picked a side — don't know enough." King flexed his hand, decided no bones were broken. "Eli didn't say he wouldn't sell me ammunition — two boxes of .45-90. Are you saying you won't?"

"Ain't saying. If I had any."

"Which side do you favor?"

Higginbotham laughed. "I mostly favor being alive and in business when the shooting stops." He went to his wooden cooler and brought back a side of bacon. Drawing a wickedly sharp knife once across his whetstone, he held it above the slab. "About here?"

"Fine. You're looking for more shooting, then?"

"Bound to be." He cut a two-pound chunk of bacon with one easy motion, tied it up in white paper, and brought out the beef. "Didn't nobody give you the lay of the land? How much do you know?"

"Somebody murdered C.D. Hollis. The judge and his friends didn't like him and don't care for Castelberry. Castleberry's clan didn't like him and doesn't care for the judge. None of them seem to think very much of me."

The butcher snorted. "Welcome to the middle, like the rest of us. This about the right thick for your steak? I'll need an hour to tell you the rest."

"Tell me one thing, then. Where's Mrs. Hollis?"

Higginbotham hesitated. "Friend of theirs, you said you were?" he murmured. "Well, it's no harm. Packed up and left, just after the funeral. Asked me to sell the house for her. Left by train, she did, her and them kids."

"For where?"

"That's two things. Waxahachie, she said. Brother-in-law owns a place there, she said." The older man blinked. "Say, you aren't — ?"

"How about the rest? I've got an hour."

"Not here." Higginbotham measured King again, not quite pointing the shiny knife at him. "Where'll you be after dark?"

King looked at the knife. "Sitting with my back to a good wall," he said.

The butcher nodded. He racked the knife, wrapped the steak and added a handful of stew meat and a loaf of dark crusty bread. "We'd have to figure we could trust one another," he said. "Was that a dozen eggs, or a half?"

"Six will be plenty."

Higginbotham counted six brown-shelled eggs into a little box of sawdust. He laid them with the other packages. Finally, he reached far under the counter and set out two boxes of Winchester .45-90s beside the rest.

"That'll be five dollars and forty-two cents. Even."

"I'll be staying at the Hollis house tonight. Best you knock before you lift the latchstring."

"Around eight o'clock?"
"Around eight o'clock."

Carrying his grub in a towsack, King circled past the depot, found the stationmaster, and sent a telegram. Coming out, he made his way back to the house where he'd first stopped. Holley trotted out from under the porch to greet him.

"It'll be a minute," King said, and went inside.

The house still smelled of lilac powder and children no cleaner than they ought to be. King had never seen the boys, although he knew a lot about them — C.D. Junior would be almost nine now, Travis just past six. He tried to picture the family, but only Rachel's face would come clear for him.

He dumped grub and saddlebags on the kitchen table and walked through the house again. Kitchen, front room, bedroom, all looking as if they'd just been used and the owners would return any second. That was all of the house except for a shed-roofed and enclosed back porch. From the signs, he figured the boys had slept there. He latched that back screen and bolted the door to the kitchen.

Rachel Hollis had taken away her boys and their clothes and very little else. King's footsteps echoed in the house, and he wished she had stayed a little longer. But Crow had shown him the knot of dried flowers she'd left on C.D.'s grave. And King knew where to find her when he was finished in Willow Springs.

He put half the stew meat into a gravy bowl and broke two of the eggs over it. Setting the bowl out for the dog, he sliced a couple of strips of bacon for the skillet, built up a fire in the stove, and worked the hand pump in the kitchen until the water was clear enough to drink. He added coffee from his saddlebags, drinking his first cup while the steak sizzled in the pan.

Out front, Holley growled. King set aside the cup and reached for his carbine. Someone trod heavily on the front porch and tapped at the front door. King's watch read seven-thirty.

"It's not locked," he said. Stepping to the kitchen doorway, he leveled the carbine and waited.

"Caw! Caw-haw-haw!" Crow stared brightly at King and the Winchester. "Didn't mean to surprise you, caw-haw! Reckon you're a mighty sudden feller. So says they all in town. Mighty sudden."

"Sorry, Cuervo. Come in."

The little man hopped nimbly inside, closing the door behind him. "Thank'ee. Mr. Drumm, him down at the depot, he says bring you this right off." He held out a tightly folded square of yellow paper. "Answer to your telegram, he says. Mighty smart feller, Mr. Drumm. Lots of smart fellers hereabouts, caw-haw."

King unfolded the telegram. *King, Willow Springs,* it said. *Take morning train, meet me same place. Slater.* He read it twice, then tucked it away.

"Thanks, Crow." He offered a coin. "Stay for a bite of steak?"

"Oh, no. Mr. Drumm done paid me. And I thank'ee, but I got to be about my doings."

"Pretty late to be working," King said.

"Some jobs best done at night. Sheriff Hollis, he thought so too." He opened the door, then looked back at King with round, serious eyes. "You take care now. Town's a dangerous place. Mighty dangerous for sudden fellers, caw-haw."

Chapter 6

November 19, 1894

From the dark shelter of a cottonwood's trunk, Cy Timm watched Buck Parnell mount the front porch of his brother's house. Timm trembled, unsure how he would explain his presence if anyone should catch him snooping. But Buck had lied about the bean. Buck had drawn a white bean, and then he'd lied.

Timm barely restrained a jump when Buck knocked lightly on the door frame. As if she'd been waiting, Sheila Parnell opened the door at once.

"Why, Buck," she said. "I thought sure it was Eli. If you're looking for him, I just don't know where he could be."

Lamplight picked up golden highlights in her red hair and painted a flush on her cheeks. She was in her nightdress, her shoulders modestly covered with a shawl; but Timm couldn't help noticing the gown was so thin that the light showed the shape of her limbs as she moved. Her voice held a note of quiet laughter.

"Eli should be home any minute," she said. "Why don't you come in and wait."

"Thanks. I don't mind if I do."

Buck stepped inside and closed the door. Lamplight threw two dark silhouettes on the shade, facing each other. As Timm watched, the two merged to form a single shadow, and then the hall lamp went out.

Dear Eli. Timm shook his head. That wouldn't do. *Friend Eli.* No, too personal. *Mr. Eli Parnell.* Better. And he would sign it *A Friend.* What troubled him was the part in between. How could he write down what he had seen and what he suspected? And suppose Eli should recognize his hand? What with his work at the courthouse, a lot of people knew his handwriting.

"Out kind of late, Cy. Felt like a walk, did you?"

Timm jumped convulsively, twisted in the air, thrust his hand into his coat pocket as he came down.

"Don't! Not likely you could hurt anybody with your toy pistol. But I might not take the chance."

Timm squeezed the hook handle of the small revolver in his pocket until his knuckles ached, trying to stop trembling. His heart hammered. Just at the edge of the street, not six feet away, Sheriff C.D. Hollis sat astride a perfectly black horse and looked down at Cy Timm. Aside from the two of them, the dark town square seemed utterly deserted.

"God of Mighty!" Timm breathed. "That must

be the quietest horse in the world!"

Hollis sat like a cat on a limb, one gloved hand just touching his holstered pistol. "Quiet as any mouse, Cy," he said. "Quieter than some."

"Do — ?" Timm heard his voice rising and clamped down tight on it. "Do you mean to shoot me?"

"Might be. It might help if you'd show your right hand empty."

Now, Timm thought. I could do it now. No nonsense about beans or shotguns. Just pull the little revolver and fire. Nobody would doubt Hollis had threatened him. Just shoot. Self-defense. Just pull and fire, right into Hollis's watchful face. Pull and fire.

Timm shivered in the wind and brought his hand out of his pocket, palm up and empty. Hollis chuckled softly.

"You've got more sand than a man might think, Cy. That was a smart move. Mighty smart man we've got for county clerk."

"What do you want?"

"Just wondering why a smart man like you is out in a norther at midnight. The way you're slipping around, a man might think you're bent on murder."

"No!" Timm caught himself. "No. I couldn't sleep. I was just — walking."

C.D. Hollis drew back on the reins, causing the black horse to shake his head against the pressure. "You don't walk. You sneak. You scurry like a mouse and spy on your friends."

Anger burned through Timm, anger mixed with shame. For an instant, he almost plunged his hand back into his pocket, ready to take Hollis on. Then he remembered the plan. *I'll do it. It's God's providence gave me that bean. I'll kill that son of a bitch or die!* Straight-backed, he faced Hollis.

"It's a cold night, Sheriff. If you don't mean to shoot me, I'm going home." He spun around and took three angry steps before looking back. "So far as sneaking goes, there's nobody in the world can touch you and that devil horse."

Hollis threw back his head. His laughter rang across the empty square. "True enough, Cy," he admitted. "Something for you to remember — if you go looking for my back in the dark."

He spoke to the horse and it glided silently back to the south, out of Timm's sight. Hollis didn't pause before Eli Parnell's house, where a respectable lamp glowed in the parlor. At the corner of the fence, he drew his pistol and fired once into the air. The report woke echoes from the sleeping mesas. Eli Parnell's bulldog barked wildly, and more dogs joined in from near and far. Smiling, C.D. Hollis rode quietly on into the darkness.

Chapter 7

December 4, 1894

Jeff King paid another day on his horses at the livery yard and bought a ticket on the eastbound train. The first coach was crowded with travelers from El Paso and beyond, but he found a seat in the next. Settling back with his carbine tucked up against the wall, he tilted his hat over his eyes and waited.

Presently the conductor drew up the iron steps. The locomotive spun its wheels, caught traction, finally lurched forward like a desert centipede uncoiling until the different segments became a single smoothly rolling unit.

King felt the power of the engine thrust him back against the seat. As the train curved out of Willow Springs toward the rising sun, he sat up and gazed out the window. Except for the evenly spaced flash of telegraph poles, all trace of civilization had ended at the edge of town. Desert scrub blurred past with monotonous sameness. A herd of antelope spooked from their grazing raced beside the engine in fluid bounds, staying even for two hundred yards before veering away into the brush.

Foolish as sheep, King thought, chasing the wind. Foolish as men! Then he frowned. The thought wasn't his, not his sort of thought even. It was something that Higginbotham had put into his head the night before.

King had been through with supper and ready for bed by the time Higginbotham's knock finally came. He had let the grocer in and listened to him — up until the part about the sheep, anyway.

King started by warming the rest of the coffee. He poured two cups and shoved one across the table to the older man.

"You said there was going to be shooting. I wish you'd tell me more about that."

"There's already been some shooting." Higginbotham looked at his cup. "Got any sugar?"

"Sorry."

"Hollis killed Donny Castleberry. Then somebody killed Hollis. There'll be more shooting. Neither side will quit now."

"You figure Hollis was on the town's side against Castleberry?"

"Let's don't call it the *town's side.*"

"The Parnells' side then. Or Blankenship's."

"Them. And others, but —"

"Who else?"

"— not the whole town. They got Hollis elected. He was their man."

"You didn't vote?"

"Sure. I voted for Hollis myself. But he danced to Blankenship's fiddle."

"I wonder would you've said that in this house when he was alive."

Higginbotham stared over the rim of his steaming cup. "Hollis, you mean? He knew what I thought."

"Well, *I* don't know what you think. You tell me there's two sides fixing to have a war — I can see that myself — and then you say Hollis was a hired killer for one of them. I damn well don't believe it."

The grocer snorted and put down his cup. "No offense, son. Here's the truth then." His voice was as sharp as his bacon knife. "Castleberry? He don't want to fence in this whole county — including the town — and call it his. No he don't! And the judge and the Parnells and old Cy Timm? They aren't trying to grab up his ranch a section at a time all legal-like. No sir, they aren't. Nobody that looked would find a bunch of county survey stakes on Castleberry's land. And Hollis? Hollis wasn't in on it — not much! He just shot Donny Castleberry to even up the odds."

"What the hell are you talking about?"

"I'm spinning you a fairy tale, seeing's that's what you'd rather hear."

The old man had sand. King studied his eyes. "So that's the way it lies, is it? Castleberry wants more land, and the judge wants the land Castleberry has."

"Pretty close. The judge wants more than that, I expect. He sees himself in the legislature, maybe even governor. Castleberry just sees himself. His land and cattle, they're part of him. Us in the way he didn't see at all. But now that he don't have his boy to carry on for him, he sees us. He blames the town because of Donny, and it'll be a burr under his blanket till he dies."

King believed that. "You said Hollis killed young Castleberry to even the odds."

Higginbotham nodded. "I was mad. But that's the way it looked." He poured himself the rest of the coffee. "Donny was a hellion. Just like his old man at twenty, I expect — hell with the ladies and good with a gun and not inclined to be pushed. He could've killed any four men face to face."

"I hope you're not saying C.D. shot him in the back."

"No. Half the night crowd saw it. Just that Donny was the second best man with a gun. Hell, if Hollis was such a special friend of yours, you ought to know *he* was the best."

I should have known it, King thought. *I would have known if I hadn't stayed away — if I'd acted like a brother should.*

"So when you heard I was a friend of Hollis, you figured I'd hire on in his place."

"Looked that way. Then we — I figured Castleberry must have offered you more money."

King smiled. "Is it money you're offering me to stand between them when the shooting starts?"

Higginbotham drew a silver dollar out of his coat pocket and pitched it onto the table between

66

them. "That's about the best pay I could offer."
He laughed. "No, if it's money you was after,
one or the other of them would have bought you
on the square this afternoon."

King took the dollar. "That's because they
didn't offer enough. This'll do."

"The hell you say!"

"I'm easy bought. What about you? I'll give
you back this dollar if you'll answer me one
question."

Higginbotham didn't like it.

"Tell me who killed C.D. Hollis," King said
quietly. He dropped the heavy coin into the
butcher's cup.

"Hell," the old man said.

"You going to drink your coffee or answer my
question?"

"Who are you?"

"I'm a man born without patience."

"If I knew the answer," Higginbotham said, "I
expect I'd already be dead. But I don't know."

"Did you do it?"

"Not likely!" Higginbotham flushed beet red
— with anger, King thought, not with shame. "I
never killed —"

"That's a start. We know one who didn't do
it. Now. Who does that leave most likely?"

The old man was sweating like a beet in a stew
pan. "Listen, I — I wouldn't like to guess about
a thing like that."

"Neither would I."

Higginbotham stood up and leaned across the

little table. He spoke very quietly. "It could have been any of them from the ranch."

"Castleberry's?"

The old man winced at the loudness of King's voice. He nodded. "I don't mean Dallas his own self. But sheep follow."

"Sheep?"

"Sheep follow. They'll follow the one in front. Right over a cliff."

"Why would the one in front run off a cliff?"

"Because while's he was trying to please his boss, he wouldn't see it."

"Sheep are easy bought, are they?"

"Listen," Higginbotham started. The dark color came into his cheeks again. "I'm sorry to trouble you. I shouldn't have come here."

King took out his watch. "You should have come — at eight o'clock. Where were you?"

"I — working."

"Working late in your store?"

"That's true. I —"

"And were you working late in your store the night that Hollis was killed?"

"No, I wasn't. What are you getting at?" Higginbotham pushed himself up from the table. "I'm leaving. I only hope I'm —"

"— not troubling you," the woman's voice said again. The chime of it brought King back to the train coach and the passing desert and the sweet warm scent of heliotrope perfume. A young woman stood in the aisle beside his seat. She couldn't have been much past twenty-one. She wore a chaste green traveling suit that fit her slender body perfectly. The strands of hair that showed beneath her bonnet shone soft and red and thick as a fox's winter coat. Her small, tilted nose looked as if it should be freckled, but it wasn't.

"Beg your pardon, Ma'am." King rose quickly, nodded to the young woman, and struck his head on the overhead rack.

She put a hand to her mouth to hide a smile, but she couldn't hide the sparkle in her eyes. "Oh, dear," she said. A faint bird-cry of laughter echoed in her voice. "I'm afraid I *am* troubling you!"

"Not at all, Ma'am," King said. "I'm afraid I was thinking of something else when you spoke. Can I help you?"

Watching him rub his head, she laughed. The bright chirp reminded King of a falcon's call. "I hope you'll forgive me for being so forward, Mr. King, but I believe you've met my husband. Since there's no one to introduce us, I'm Sheila Parnell."

"My pleasure, Mrs. Parnell," King said cautiously. That explained how she knew his name, but it made him wonder why she would be civil. "You'd be the sheriff's wife, then."

The young woman looked startled. Then she gave him a warm smile. "That's my fault," she murmured. "I should have said that I'm Mrs. Eli Parnell. Since I'm forced to travel alone, I was hoping you'd be my protector."

"I see," King said. He didn't. He stopped himself from rolling the brim of his hat and nodded again. "I'd be honored to have you join me."

Sheila Parnell looked at him from beneath long lashes. "Thank you, Mr. King. I was sure you were a gentleman." She nestled into the aisle seat and waited while he bent past the rack to resume his place. "I'm sorry you didn't like Willow Springs. You didn't even spend a whole day with us."

"Still making up my mind."

"Oh?" She gestured vaguely. "But you're on your way to Austin City." Her face was a question as she looked up at him. "Aren't you? When I saw you here, I supposed . . ." She allowed her eyes to fall as her words trailed off.

Suddenly, King understood. Sweet, pretty, flirtatious Sheila Parnell had come to watch him, to find out what he was up to. There was nothing like a pretty face to bring out the fool in a man, he told himself. But there was some excuse when the face was as beautiful as this one.

"It'll be a pleasure to have such a charming traveling companion," he said. "You're going to Austin City, then?"

"Why, yes. To do some shopping and visit Eli's sister."

"Well, I wish I could — protect — you the whole way." He watched bright red spots glow in her cheeks at his words. "But I'll be getting off at Langtry."

70

"But —" she said. "Oh, I'm sorry. I must have misunderstood."

"I'll try to keep you safe that far," King said.

She searched his eyes for a smile. Her own face took on a deeper color. "Thank you." She straightened her skirts and spoke in a slightly harder tone. "My husband tells me you were acquainted with our former sheriff."

King was tired of playing games, tired of people toying with words. "C.D. was my brother," he said.

Sheila Parnell took that news like a bath of ice water. Her bright blue eyes widened in surprise laced with a sudden hint of fear. "But — your name isn't — I thought . . ."

"You're only half my brother!"

"His pa was killed at Shiloh. Our mother and my pa died when I was about ten. C.D. raised me until I could look after myself." King looked at the pretty falcon they'd sent to find him out. He was making it easy for her. "So you'd call him my half brother, but he was as much a brother to me as anybody could have been."

Why'd I never tell him that? Why'd he have to die before I could?

The note of wheels on rails changed to a clattering roar as the train pounded onto a trestle which spanned a deep, rock-hewn canyon. Glimpsed through the iron girders, the distant riverbed was dry and paved with boulders and gravel. The two of them stared out the window until the bridge was past. When the woman spoke

71

again, her voice was almost too soft to be heard above the rhythmic clack of the great iron wheels.

"I'm so sorry for your loss," she said. She sounded as if she meant it. Then, "It explains your staying in . . ."

"In my brother's house?"

The sudden candor of their conversation had taken away the apple blush in her cheeks. "Willow Springs is a small town," she said.

King began to like her better. "I'd guess you don't come from a small town."

She smiled. "No, I was reared in St. Louis. I met Mr. Parnell when he came there on a buying trip."

"And he wooed and won you and brought you home to Willow Springs with him."

"Almost, yes." She looked into King's eyes, daring him to laugh. After a moment, she went on as if the direction of their conversation had gotten away from her and no longer mattered. "Later he sent his brother back to St. Louis to accompany me on the train to Willow Springs."

"That'd be Buck?" It was a story King had heard somewhere, sometime — the older man sending a younger to fetch his bride. But he couldn't remember where he had heard it or when.

"Yes." She looked again to see whether he was laughing at her. "Yes, that's what happened." She smiled gently. "Do you have other kin in Langtry, Mr. King?"

"Kin? No, just business."

The word business seemed to remind Sheila Parnell of something. She looked at King's things in the seat ahead of them. "Business?" she said. Teasingly, she leaned forward and put her little finger down the bore of his .45-90 carbine. "Do you always do business with that big gun, Mr. King?"

"Very often." When she moved, King caught the smell of heliotrope. The pleasant scent almost kept him from saying more. "I wouldn't put my finger there if I were you, Mrs. Parnell."

"Wouldn't you?" She lowered her head to gaze at him still teasingly through the fringe of her lashes. "I'd thought of you as a man bold enough to put his finger wherever he chose."

King shook his head. "I wouldn't do it because I know the owner keeps a round in the chamber day and night."

"He must be a very dangerous man, the owner."

If King had been doubtful, now he was certain. *She's been sent,* he thought. *The devil's falcon, sent to fetch me.* She could seem as shamelessly forward as a saloon harlot one moment and chastely reserved the next. King took it as a hint that Sheila Parnell was offering less of herself than a man might believe. He shook his head again. "No," he said. "The owner's like the carbine — just dangerous to handle."

In Langtry, Jeff King tipped his hat to Sheila Parnell, gathered his gear, and left the train. He didn't need to look back to feel her watching him, but he did. Their eyes held with neither smile nor frown until the train had drawn her out of sight. It came to him that he might have been wrong. She might be offering more of herself than a man expected.

He shook his head to clear away the thought. The Langtry railroad station didn't amount to much, no more than a yellow-painted shed fronted by a rickety wooden platform.

Close by the shed stood a broad man waiting on the platform, meditatively studying the toes of his boots. King strode past him without a look and trotted down the far steps.

To the south of the tracks a wide, rough slope led down into the bottomlands of the Rio Grande. The banks of the river were thickly grown with willows and cane and cottonwoods that hid all but glimpses of the swirling brown water. Beyond the river rose the mountains of Mexico. King looked thoughtfully toward those mountains for a moment, then turned and walked to the scatter of buildings that was Langtry, Texas.

Set a little apart from the rest, one wooden shack bore a festoon of signs, the largest announcing with more enthusiasm than accuracy that it was The Jersey Lilly. King mounted the sagging porch and pushed through the door.

The place was dim and dirty-looking. King stopped to wait for his eyes to adjust from the bright sunlight outside. Half a dozen men measured him and his carbine and his stance before going back to their own business. The elderly, slope-shouldered bartender cocked his head and stared at King.

"I know you, Bub," he said.

King laid a quarter on the bar. "Not likely," he said. "I'll have one of those iced beers you advertise."

The bartender stroked his scraggly white beard. "Fact is we're plumb out of ice. Got the beer, and it's cool enough this time of year."

"Thanks." King took the brown bottle to a corner table, dumped his saddlebags on a chair, and leaned the carbine against his knee. A mile down the line, the Austin City train let go a mournful whistle. Jeff King was afoot a long way from home.

He looked around the room, recognizing no one from Willow Springs. Only the bartender seemed to take any interest in him. Then the front door opened, and a cold wind came in with the man from the station platform. Square and dark, he seemed all coat, hat, and eyes. He studied the room as King had done, bought tobacco at the bar, and went purposefully outside again.

"Well, hell," King sighed. He picked up his bottle and his gear and followed.

Outside, the square man stood on the porch, facing into the brisk south wind, cupping one big hand around a match to get his pipe going. He took three matches. Then he bit down on the stem and spoke through his teeth.

"King," was all he said, but it was *Hello* and *Good to see you* and *How did things go on the border?* all in one word.

"Captain," King answered. It was *How the hell are you, John?* and *The job's done* and *What about that telegram?*

They shook hands. Then the door opened quickly, and the white-bearded owner slipped outside, holding two more brown bottles by their necks.

"Captain Slater," he said to the square man. "Good to have you back at the Lilly. These two are on the house for you and your Ranger boy." He held out the bottles. "When I said I knew you," he told King, "you denied it. You ought never to doubt me on knowing a man's face, whether you're wearing your badge or not."

"Roy," the square man said, "Jeff and I just need to perch on your stoop for a spell. Got some official things to talk about."

"Got somebody needs hanging?"

"Not yet. Maybe later," Slater said. "We'd sure appreciate it if you'd see to it nobody listens in."

"You bet. You can count on Roy Bean!"

"Thanks, Judge." Slater waited until Bean was gone and the door firmly shut behind him. Then he leaned on the porch railing and looked at King. "I hate it about C.D.," he said. "We joined the Ranger service together. Rode together, drank together, wenched together, chased outlaws and horse thieves and bronco Apache to-gether."

"Yeah."

"Hell and damnation!" Slater puffed a cloud of smoke like a black-powder cannon. "He'd be captain in my place if he'd stayed in, but he had to go off like he did. I never knew why."

King said nothing. He set his bottle on the wooden railing and turned to look across the tracks toward the river. Slater didn't seem to notice.

"Then to let one of those yellow toads in Willow Springs cut him down — and with a shotgun! He must have slipped from what he used to be." Slater saw the look on King's face and stood up suddenly. "Hell. Pardon me, Sergeant. I'd forgot he was half your brother."

"He was all my brother!" They watched each other until the pain was past. "I want all of his killer."

"Don't worry." Slater nodded grimly, still looking at King with hooded eyes. "I expect I'll handle that job myself." He pulled a train ticket from his breast pocket and slapped it down on the rail. "Here's your ticket back to Austin City. Let me have your return passage to Willow Springs."

King didn't take time to consider. The beer bottle was in his hand, and he flung it straight through the front window of The Jersey Lilly. Glass and framing crashed inside, and a blur of excited voices poured out through the airy opening. When King brought his other hand down on Slater's ticket, he left a silver star with a ring around it.

"Sell the silver," he said roughly, "and buy your own ticket."

"Now — by the Law! — what's all this racket?" Bean's whiskered face appeared at the door with the other patrons clustered behind him. "That window don't come free, Rangers or no! You know what a piece of glass costs out here? I got a mind to convene court right now!"

"I'll take care of it, Roy," Slater said. "Go on along, now." To King he said, "Pick up that badge. I won't have another of you damned East Texas farm boys quit on me! And that glass'll come out of your pay."

King saw that Slater felt as guilty about Hollis as he did. But it didn't matter. "I don't have any pay, and I've already quit."

"I don't want you underfoot."

"Doesn't matter what you want. I'm going back."

"Why hell." Slater looked through the open window into the bar. "We're just wasting time. I knew that'd be the way of it, was you C.D.'s true brother." Slater smiled about it. "And I guess you are. Sudden-tempered, stud born, and cranky as a ram goat! You're his blood, all right."

"I'll see you." King turned away.

"Now wait. Just wait up. I'll let you go nasty but I won't let you go stupid."

"You don't have anything to do with it."

"Well, now, I wish you hadn't said that." Slater set his bottle on the rail, laid his pipe beside it, and unbuttoned his coat. "But I'm still going to leave you a choice."

King waited.

"Pick up your badge, listen to what I've come to tell you, and go back to Willow Springs real official-like."

"Or?"

"Or I'll turn you over to Bean to stand trial for breaking his window." He raised a hand as King started to speak. "I'll do exactly that to keep you out of it unless you take back that badge right now. I know your feelings, but I mean business."

King decided he did. "All right." He picked up his badge.

"Come away from the window and sit down. The next westbound won't be here for a couple of hours. Now. You'll want to read this." Captain Slater offered King a well-handled envelope. The envelope and letter were addressed to the Adjutant General, State of Texas, Austin. The date was more than a week past. King frowned at the spidery script.

Esteemed Sir:

I beg you to dispatch a force of Rangers to arrest the murderer of Sheriff Hollis. I think it best not to write down names, but five citizens of Willow Springs have connived his death. Four drew white beans. The drawer of the black was to kill Hollis with a shotgun. Their purpose was to do the killing at a time when all would be out of the way or have witnesses to show their innocence. The real killer did not await the appointed time, but instead shot Hollis that very night.

It was I who drew the fatal black bean. But I did not do the killing! I was at first glad someone had lifted that burden from me, but I soon saw my mistake. By killing him out of time, some one of our number means to destroy all the rest. I fear to name him or myself. When your Rangers come, I will reveal all in the hope of forgiveness. I beg your excellency — act quickly.
                              Your Obedient Servant.

"Well," Slater asked, "what do you think of our rat? Reckon there's a word of truth to it?"

"I'd bet pay on it." King refolded the letter and put it inside his coat. "I've got the ears notched on four of them already, sure as you're a foot high."

"Don't let that fifth one get behind you! You got any proof?"

"Enough."

"Enough to suit you or to suit a judge?"

King thought that funny. "I'll get proof and I'll nail the fifth one."

"Ummm." Slater drew his pipe back to life. "Why do you reckon a man would be downright sheep-dumb enough to *ask* us to come and get

80

him? Something doesn't add."

"Right there in the letter," King said. "He *hopes* the law'll forgive him. He *knows* his cronies won't."

"If that's the case, you'll have to figure him out before they do. Else he's not apt to tell you much. He one of the four you got marked?"

"Chances are." *Four chances in five,* he thought.

"I don't like it." Slater straightened and took a turn around the porch, frowning at the floor with every step. "Seems to me you're likely to be the object of their next bean drawing."

King laughed and rested a palm on the butt of his pistol. "They can try," he said.

"I don't like that, either. That's about what C.D. must have said. Listen, Jeff, let's work this thing together, so's to watch each other's backs."

"Give me two weeks to do it myself."

"Two seconds is enough to get yourself killed."

"Give me a week from Sunday."

Slater sighed. "I'll give you a week from right now." He looked at his watch. "If you haven't scratched by then, I'm coming into Willow Springs with enough help to sift this thing. Enough help to jail you, too, if you get in my way."

"That's not much time."

"Suit yourself. It's all you're going to get."

Chapter 8

November 19, 1894

C.D. Hollis tied his horse in the shadows near the courthouse. Easing into a sheltered corner, he took out his pocketknife and scraped the scale from the bowl of his pipe. Packing it with Half and Half, he cupped a match to the bowl and settled in to think.

The night was raw and Rachel warm in their bed at home. He could be there with her, he knew, but for his hunter's joy in the stalk and his hurt pride.

Is that all it comes to — just pride? Maybe so. Like that time with Jeff Davis, when they'd both been wrong and too proud to own up. This time, he'd imagined the judge had wanted him for his reputation as a lawman. All the time, he'd been a tool — no more than a hand to pull a trigger — to be used and thrown away.

They did a murder, the black and clever bastards. A murder, and I was the weapon. He tapped the pipe against the wall and watched bright sparks dance away on the wind. *Why hasn't Dallas come to kill me?*

The answer came to him on the wind.

He's smarter, that's all. He knows they set it up — the judge and his cronies. Coming for me, he'd be finishing their work. I'd take him down, too, or they'd send for the Rangers and hang him.

That had to be right. Dallas Castleberry had seen down the road, even that first day with Donny lying dead at the undertaker's.

He saw I had the loop off my hammer, expecting him to try. And didn't he have his vaqueros to back him up? Didn't he have to fight himself back from it? Even then, he knew better. He's always been the smart one. That's why I needed him.

Hollis shook his head impatiently. Too late for that now. Castleberry was playing his own game. His was a tough breed, tough as the longhorns he'd raised. He wasn't beaten, but there was no knowing what was in his mind.

Well, I'm not beaten, either. They figured to get rid of me before I worked it out, but I've made them dance a little. And they don't know I've already sent for a Ranger, unofficial like. What the geese don't know won't hurt the gander. About the time Jeff and me both get after them, they'll think I'm smarter than I seem.

There it was, the way out of his trouble. With a little luck, he'd see the lot of them behind bars. Then he could get John Slater to give him his old badge back, and Castleberry would have to back off or face the whole Ranger corps. Hollis grinned. He'd pull through yet. He always had, in spite of everything — in spite of his own folly.

Good thing God don't show people a fool's thoughts.

The pipe bit at his tongue. In his reverie, he'd drawn on it until the tobacco was one glowing coal. He started to shake it out, but froze at the sudden sound of a door opening. A man emerged from the courthouse into the moonlit shadows. Hollis laid the pipe aside, drew open his coat to expose badge and pistol, and walked in that direction.

"Blankenship!"

Blankenship started and whirled around, his hand disappearing inside his coat.

"That's fine," Hollis said, striding steadily toward him. "Just like your mouse. Go ahead and do it."

Go ahead. Pull that little Smoot Patent Pocket Pistol out in the open. I'll put your heart through your backbone and end your part of this.

As if God had shown him a fool's thoughts, the judge withdrew his hand. "Good evening, Sheriff," he said quietly. "You startled me, out so late. I thought I heard something earlier — a shot?"

"It was. I've taken care of it."

"I see. We in Willow Springs are indeed lucky to have such a devoted lawman watching over us."

"That's God's truth, even if you don't mean a word of it." Hollis stepped closer, letting his size push Blankenship back a step. He stared at the judge with the power of truth and law and justice

84

on his side. "Remember to tell that to the devil when you get to hell."

"Since you don't want to be civil, I'll remind you I can have you up on charges. You'd hate to lose that badge you hide under your coat."

"This one?" Hollis drew back the long coat again. He counted a point for Blankenship; his time in the Rangers had taught him not to show a badge until it was needed. "Try taking it if it suits you. Could be when the dust clears, we'll neither of us have a job." He grinned. "But I know where to find another badge. What would you do, Judge?"

Blankenship's face hardened. "I'm not afraid of you," he said coldly. "First thing in the morning —"

"You don't understand me," Hollis interrupted softly — so softly that Blankenship had no warning until Hollis's left hand smashed into the arch of his ribs and doubled him over. While he was still trying to breathe, a hard right behind the ear drove him down on the sand at the sheriff's feet.

"Pay attention," Hollis continued, still softly. "I never thought you were afraid. You're a brave enough man, for all that you're a liar and a thief who used me to do your killing."

The judge rolled to his knees, raising his hand to the side of his head. He stared dully at the blood on his fingers, then took out a handkerchief and pressed it against his ear.

"Are you listening, Judge? This is no threat.

When I get the proof I need, I mean to take you down, whether you're lording it over your courtroom or running away. It'll all be the same."

Blankenship looked up at him steadily. "You'll not live that long," he said.

"I might. There's a Ranger coming to look into Donny Castleberry's killing."

"Your killing, Hollis, not mine."

"We'll see. Understand me — you're going to lose that office you love so much. Maybe you're going to jail. And if you'd like to hang —" He paused and grinned at Blankenship's livid face. "If you'd like to hang, why, just let something happen to me."

Chapter 9

December 5, 1894

Court was in session in Blackrock County when Jeff King reached the courthouse next day. He stepped inside the courtroom and looked for an empty pew nearby, then settled for standing at the back.

The morning was chilly, so King had picked up C.D.'s old fleece-lined coat. It was a bit tight across the shoulders, but it fit him well enough. He would have taken it off but he saw no place to hang it.

Although in such small details as coat racks, it was yet unfinished, the new court was impressive. Rich, dark wood paneling ran head high round the entire room. The vaulted ceiling, set with iron-framed skylights, gave the place a feel of space and grandeur. Oak chairs and tables and benches provided seating for attorneys and spectators; but the jury box and the judge's tall bench were paneled in the same wood as the walls.

On that day, every seat was taken. King caught the tense expectancy that meant the end of a trial. Twelve grim men dressed in their black-suited best filled the jury box. At the prosecution table, the state's attorney relaxed, hands in his pockets, while across the room a man in a plaid suit sat with his elbows braced on the table and his forehead resting on his clenched fists. The prisoner, a stocky Mexican man, frowned attentively toward the judge's bench, where Sheriff Buck Parnell stood with folded arms beneath the Texas flag. Dark and solemn as the shadow of death in his judicial robes, Judge Blankenship was speaking.

"— have been found guilty of the crime of murder. Nor was it a murder fueled by the heat of anger or driven on by the lash of passion. Instead, it was the cowardly and cold-blooded slaying of a man who trusted you, who had every claim upon your friendship."

He paused for an impressive moment, staring down at the prisoner. The man stared back, a little frown creasing his forehead. King didn't think he understood much of what the judge was saying, but that didn't deprive Blankenship of his moment.

"Though it is a heavy burden to pronounce the sentence of death upon a fellow man, circumstances sometimes require it. The ancient Greeks said, 'The judge is condemned when the criminal is absolved.' The facts of this case speak for themselves." He drew in his breath and swept an imperious glance across the crowd. "Jesus Bustamente Gonzalez, I hereby sentence you —"

Then Judge Blankenship's eyes fell on the bulky figure at the back of the room, on the turned-up collar of the leather coat, on the steady eyes that watched him. For an instant, the judge froze in midsentence. Color seeped from his proud face, and his pale lips twisted into a single silent word.

Hollis!

Probably no one but King understood the word, though Buck Parnell was looking anxiously from the judge to the crowd and back. Almost at once, before even the first puzzled whisper could start, the judge caught himself.

"Jesus Bustamente Gonzalez," he repeated, his eyes still locked on King, "I sentence you to — to the term of ten years in the Texas state penitentiary. Sheriff, take the prisoner."

The plaid-suited lawyer raised his head to gape at the judge. The state's attorney was on his feet, shouting words lost in the babble of jury and spectators. But Judge Homer Blankenship had already slammed his gavel down and moved swiftly toward his chambers.

King watched the heavy door close with a slam. Then he grinned in slow understanding. *Smart fellows, those Greeks,* he thought as he turned to leave the courtroom. *They must've had ideas on mighty near everything. Wonder what they'd say about the judge. I'll have to ask him.*

At the public stable, he roused the sleepy hostler and asked for his horses. His mind was still on judges and justice in Blackrock County.

"You say you want them both saddled?" Young, skinny, and too long for his clothes, the boy hadn't moved from his stool. "Which one you aim to ride?"

"Cinch them both tight so I can ride whichever suits me. And I'd like to get started today, if it's no trouble. Put the new saddle on the black."

"Mighty like Sheriff Hollis's horse, that black," the boy said. "Mighty like."

"What became of Sheriff Hollis's black?"

"Oh, he's in back. We board him and pasture him here. Belongs to Mr. Timm now." Rubbing a hand through his thatch of hair, the boy laughed. "Don't know what an old stick like him wanted with that horse. He's scared to ride him."

"You never know what's in another man's mind," King murmured. "Get 'em saddled, son."

Once in motion, the hostler worked swiftly and with assurance. In a surprisingly short time, he led out both horses and gave King their reins. "Thanks for the business, mister," he said. Somebody had trained him pretty well. "Come again."

"I'll do that. Save me a stall."

King swung aboard the roan and led the prancing black out into the cold sunlit morning. Just past the door, Buck Parnell stepped out to block his way.

"Mr. King," he said. He planted his feet and hooked his thumbs in his belt. "I voted to hang you straight away, just on general principles. Judge said no. He wants to see you in his chambers right about now."

"Sorry." King guided the roan past. "I've got

90

other business. I'll be around to call on the judge later. You tell him he can count on it."

King expected an argument. Instead, Buck stepped aside and grinned up at him.

"I'll do just that, friend. He ain't used to waiting for people. Most likely it'll do him good to learn." Then the grin tightened into a look of cool, level speculation. "There's some of us around here don't believe in ghosts. You might want to remember that before you make any more mistakes."

"There must be some who weren't surprised I favor C.D.," King said. "Wonder who might have mentioned we were kin?"

Buck's grin faded. "Wonder if you're really as stupid as you act, friend?" His hand dropped to his holster. "Could be you've made that mistake."

King twitched the reins. The roan tossed its head, forcing Buck back a step. He recovered quickly, but when he raised his head, he was staring straight into the wide bore of King's carbine.

King rested the short barrel across the saddlebow and thumbed back the hammer. "Anybody can make that one last mistake, Sheriff. Don't you make it now."

Buck swallowed, staring at King and the Winchester. He was thinking it over, King knew. He might have taken a chance on drawing as he ducked or twisted away but for Eli's sharp voice.

"Buck!"

"Stay clear," Buck said without looking at his brother. "It's between him and me."

"No!" Eli Parnell came quickly across the street. "It's not just you. It's all of us. The reputation of the whole town."

King watched the brothers a moment before he set his horse in motion. "I'll leave the reputation of the town in your hands," he told them. Then he kicked the roan's flanks and set off at a trot towing the black behind.

"What were you thinking?" Eli demanded.

Buck kept his eyes on King's back as the Ranger rode straight on toward the south, toward Castleberry's ranch. "Just like Hollis. He's got to die."

"No! That's exactly wrong. We can't stand another killing. Just remember you don't have a black bean for King! You can't go off on your own hook. Like as not it'd put all our necks in a noose!"

Buck looked at his older brother. "And what the hell do you figure King'll do with our necks if we *don't* kill him?"

Jeff King seated the carbine in his saddle boot and took the curving road south out of town. Dallas Castleberry had meant what he said about his ranch being easy to find. Barely a hundred yards south of the last Willow Springs dwelling, the DC boundary loomed for everyone to see. A six-strand barbed wire fence ran left and right as straight as a carpenter's chalkline through the scrub and dry grass across low swelling hills and up the sides of the distant mesas until its track was lost in the vastness of the basin.

The only break King could see in the infinite reach was the barred metal gate that seemed to block the county road. But at the last possible moment, the public road swerved off to the east to run parallel with that fence. The ranch road ran smoothly ahead to the gate. A single loop of chain held the gate closed. There was no lock but a neatly lettered wooden sign hung from the crossbar to warn the literate: Castleberry Land — Keep Out.

King rode up to open the gate, passed through, and closed it behind him. For the first mile or so, he tried to keep a count of the cattle bunched here and there to browse on the tall dry grass. Finally, he gave up. He had not yet come in sight of the ranch headquarters when he noticed his escort.

Off to the west, just out of what they might think was rifle range, two vaqueros rode slowly through the milling cattle. When he saw they were keeping pace with him, King looked to the east where three more riders paralleled his course in the same fashion. Dallas Castleberry was a careful man.

The closer King came to the cluster of buildings ahead, the more the brush opened out around him. The valley had been cleared. Under the weak December sunlight, the grass lay stiff and colorless, but still rich in the nourishment that kept the cattle and the ranch alive. To many the valley would hold no beauty at the moment. In season, however, it would be a lush green bowl with white buildings and fences standing at its center. King kept on toward the distant buildings.

A horse and buggy came out of the headquarters and flung out along the road in King's direction. From its speed, he guessed the driver was Diana Castleberry. He guided his horse off the road and waited.

From the look of her, Diana might indeed have intended to run King down. Instead, she drew back on the reins and set the brake to skid to a stop beside him. "A fine one you are," she cried. "I've lost the whole morning waiting for you."

King tipped his hat to her.

"I could've been to town and back by now if I'd known you were such a late sleeper." Then she gave him a dazzling smile.

He wondered if she was going to be a different woman every time he met her. "Sorry to put you out," he said. "If you want to see me, why don't I ride back in with you?"

If King had been charmed by her smile, he was fascinated by the little-girl blush that followed it. "I'd like that," she said finally. "But Papa is waiting for you. You go on."

He touched his hat again and nudged his horse.

"Just be sure to stay until I get home. I mean — I'll want to show you around."

King stood down from his horse. He walked

to the buggy, put his hand on the seat rail, and looked into Diana Castleberry's dark eyes. They held the same merriment he'd noticed when she asked if he was a horse thief.

"What are you staring at?"

"Can't say. Just wanted to be sure you were the same person that pointed a gun at me yesterday. You're hard to keep up with."

Then she really did blush. She put a gloved hand on his big knuckles. "I'm sorry. I didn't know who you were. Just you wait for me. Hear?" Then she released the brake and drove away at the only speed she seemed to understand.

King shut his eyes against the dust. *I didn't know who you were.* Did that mean she knew now? He mounted and rode on, considering himself lucky. He had come to see Dallas Castleberry, to find his brother's killer, to get down to business. But if Diana had asked him, Jeff King might very well have followed her back to town. Just as well she had broken the spell.

At a corral near the main house, a dozen hands were breaking horses. Dallas Castleberry sat easily on his tall gray horse to direct the work. He saw King and reined around to watch his approach. The five vaqueros who had paced him from the ranch gate had closed in a little as he approached Castleberry. Now, at some sign from him, they turned their horses and rode back north onto the great pastures.

"Finally got here, did you?" Castleberry sang out. "Wouldn't have figured anybody could be this long finding the DC."

"I wasn't too sure of my welcome."

Dallas Castleberry looked along the road where his daughter's buggy had disappeared. "I wouldn't have thought you to be afraid of that little girl. Were her manners poor?"

King shook his head. "She's quite a lady."

"In her bloodline." Castleberry still gazed toward the horizon. "High-strung and spirited, too. She was away at school when Donny — died. The way things are, I almost wish she'd not come back. At least she didn't get here until the day after —"

He stopped short and looked sharply at King, as if he'd been speaking his thoughts aloud and suddenly remembered King was listening.

"After Hollis was killed, you mean," King said.

Castleberry looked at him a moment longer. "Yes, that's what I mean." He shook his head abruptly. "Why hell then, let's go up to the house." He waved at his men. "You boys stay after it."

He turned his horse and rode beside King toward the tall white house. A lone live oak shadowed the hitchrail. Castleberry stopped his horse — and stepped down all in one motion. Before King had dismounted, a young Mexican boy was there to take his reins.

"Thank you, Noel," the rancher said. He held out a hand toward King. "Here we are. Come in and rest your bones."

King followed him up the steps and into the

warmth of the house. Across thirty feet of flag-stone floor, a fire burned high in a great stone fireplace. Sparks cascaded up the chimney from fresh logs. Two wide leather chairs flanked the hearth. Brightly colored Mexican blankets hung like battle flags along the walls. On either side of the mantlepiece hung the heads of two black-tailed bucks that might have been twins. Off to the right loomed an arched doorway, its curtain of beaded strings still swaying from recent passage. Castleberry motioned King toward one of the chairs.

"Socorro!" he called in the direction of the doorway. "We have company. Coffee and brandy for two cold waddies."

King heard no answer, but as he shed his coat a slender, middle-aged Mexican woman came through the beads with a tray bearing a silver coffeepot, two cups, and a tall brandy bottle. Seeing King, she stopped short, and her eyes rounded in momentary surprise. Then her face smoothed into a neutral smile and she leaned gracefully to set the tray on the dark sideboard.

"Thank you," Castleberry said again. "Socorro, meet our company, Mr. Jeff King. King, this is Socorro."

She curtsied stiffly, her eyes hooded. "Ma'am," King said. Apparently, courtesies came naturally to the rancher.

"You might bring some of those sweets, if there's any left," Castleberry said.

"Sweets will spoil your lunch," the woman told

him firmly. She poured coffee with swift economy of motion, then turned in a swirl of skirts and left the room.

"Speaking of dinner, you'd best set another place," Castleberry called after her. "King will be staying." He spiked each cup with a dollop of brandy and offered one to King. "Sassy as a bobcat, that Socorro," he said with a shake of his head.

"Are all your hands Mexican?" King asked.

The rancher shot him an appraising look. "They are. Out of Chihuahua and Sonora, some of them, but most is as good a Texan as me or you." He watched for a reaction from King, then added, "Good people. They understand about loyalty, which few enough folks do nowadays. Socorro's really kept things going around here since Mrs. Castleberry's took ill."

He spoke as if the illness were some secret shame for his household. King settled into one of the leather chairs and let his glance travel around the room, looking for any sign of a woman's softening influence. From above the beaded doorway, the mounted head of a javelina glared back at him over curved shining tusks.

"I'm sorry. Has she been sick for a long time?"

Castleberry's face went darker. "She took to her bed the day we buried our son, Donny."

"I *am* sorry." King remembered what Higginbotham had told him. *After C.D. killed him, you mean. Is that coming next?*

It was. Castleberry seemed to cross some line

in his soul, a line separating him from patience and restraint. "Your friend Hollis murdered Donny, shot him down in the street in Willow Springs."

King drew in his breath. "Hollis wasn't my friend," he said slowly. "He was my brother."

Chapter 10

November 19, 1894

Buck Parnell sprang out of his brother's bed as though it had turned to hot coals. The echoes of a single pistol shot hung in the air. He snatched at his revolver and hit the floor rolling, fetching up at the window that fronted on the street. Cautiously, he edged back the shade.

"Buck! What's wrong?" Sheila sat up, clasping the sheet to her throat with both hands. Unbound, her fiery hair haloed her face and floated free to her shoulders. Her eyes were wide and frightened. "Was that a shot?"

"Yes. Get on the floor — quick! Tige, hush!"

"Buck — ?"

"Be still!"

In the distance a locomotive wailed mournfully and the steady murmur of wheels began. Buck wrinkled his forehead in concentration, searching for the nearer sounds of movement.

"He's gone."

"Who? Who would — ?"

"Who? Hollis, that's who! Who the hell else?" Rising, he snatched his pants from the foot of the bed, struggling into them without putting down the pistol. "God damn him! What's the matter, was this supposed to be *his* night?"

Sheila was on him before he could move. Her fist smashed against his cheekbone hard enough to clear his head. He blocked her second blow with an upflung forearm, then pinioned her arms with a bearhug.

"Damn you!" She kicked and writhed, sobbing in anger and frustration. "Damn you, Buck Parnell! You talk like I'm a whore, when you know good and well I love you! What does it take to prove how — ?" She broke off. Her body went still in his arms and her voice filled with fear. "Buck, he *knows!* About *us!* Sweet mother Mary, what if he tells Eli?"

"Then Eli will know the truth," Buck said. He eased his grip, but kept his arms around her. "We're the ones should tell him. We ought to be together."

"Buck, no!" She stared up at him, eyes huge. "No! I can't hurt Eli that way. And —"

"To hell with Eli."

"— if anyone finds out, I'm ruined. It's easy for you, but think what they'd say about me — and they'd be right." She caught at his arms with frantic strength. "Buck, stop him, please. Don't let him tell."

Buck looked down into her tearstained face. Then he released her and reached for his shirt. "All right," he said quietly.

"Buck?" Something in his voice frightened her. "Buck, what are you going to do?"

He was pulling on his boots. "Go back to bed, Sheila," he said. "Don't say anything about any of this. He won't tell."

Still staring at him, Sheila felt across the bed-clothes until she found her robe. She held it in front of her. "I didn't mean —" she began.

"Yes you did. Or if you didn't, it doesn't matter. Go back to bed."

"No. Oh, no." She sank down on the edge of the bed. "You mustn't. But we can't let him tell Eli."

"To hell with Eli," Buck said again. But he said it as he left the bedroom, too softly for her to hear. On his way out, he paused at the hall closet where he knew Eli kept his old 10-gauge goose gun.

Eli Parnell raised unseeing eyes from his account book, wondering what sound had roused him from his thoughts. Gently, he closed the brown leather covers. He hadn't made a single entry. His mind was on Buck. Buck was high-strung and rebellious, but maybe that was to be expected at his age. Maybe it was natural for him to chafe under an older brother's control, to strut and swagger to prove himself a man.

Buck's heart was in the right place, no doubting that. Eli remembered how willingly Buck had made the long journey to St. Louis to bring Sheila out for the wedding, how hard he'd worked to make her feel welcome in Willow Springs. Eli owed him for that. Besides, an older brother was heaven-bound to look after his kin.

Now Buck had drawn the black bean. It wasn't fair. Killing, even of a man like Hollis, was a job for someone more mature. If it had to be done, then someone less swayed by anger, less likely to be damaged, should do it — the head of the family.

With fingers clumsy as wooden blocks, Eli took two black buckshot shells from his desk. He stood them on top of the glass display case like candles in an unholy Mass while he took out a wicked little Greener stagecoach gun. In the lamplight, the twin hammers reminded him of horns. Too short for hunting game, the stubby Greener was intended to kill men at close range. Eli hated the gun, but he knew what was demanded of him. Loading the shotgun, he blew out the lamp and went to do his duty.

Henry Drumm stood on the station platform and watched the red lanterns of the ten-fifty to El Paso diminish into the night. The rattle and hiss and roar of its passage still drowned all sounds from the night outside. The train was an hour late, held up on a siding just outside of town waiting for the eastbound express — also late — to pass. No one had gotten off at Willow Springs, and Drumm was quietly relieved not to have passengers to deal with at this time of night. His day's work done, he went inside to shut down the telegraph key.

The key was where his importance lay. He

could see that certain messages were sent, others delayed. His telegrams instructed an Austin City law firm what land surveys to file on. It lay within his power, if he chose to touch the key, to summon up the Rangers, or the governor, or even President Cleveland. Blankenship and Buck Parnell thought they ruled the roost, but it was Henry Drumm who really controlled Willow Springs.

I drew a white bean, he mused. His earlier elation was gone. *Homer's smart enough so's he'd get one, too. That leaves Eli and Buck and Cy.*

Sitting in the darkened station, Drumm took out a cigar and clamped it unlit between his teeth. He leaned back in his chair and waited to see where his thoughts would take him.

Buck would do fine — though he'd rather shoot Eli. Eli's tough enough, unless that little redheaded slut has softened him up. Then there's Cy.

Drumm sat up suddenly, amazement on his face. Now he knew what bothered him. God would never pass up a chance to play a trick like that on the lot of them. Sure as God made him, Cy Timm had drawn the black bean. Thinking back, Drumm could even remember the sickly expression on the little weasel's face when he'd peered into his palm. Cy Timm had the job, and there wasn't a chance under heaven he could pull it off!

Laughing aloud, Drumm slung his green eyeshade aside and clapped on his hat. Then he poked under the counter for the railroad's shotgun. Nobody in town would think twice about his taking it home. He hadn't quite decided to use it, but the risk stirred his blood. He held the key to the whole town. No reason he should wait on someone else to do the job — and it would be a good joke on Homer and all his careful planning.

Cy Timm heard the shot. His nerves reacted against his will, flinging him straight over the Widow Gantry's low picket fence. Cowering among the shrubs in her front yard, he realized the bullet wasn't meant for him. Anger burned through his fear — anger at his own cowardly body, at his inability to control it, at Hollis for bringing out the fear in him.

For being who he is, Timm thought with sudden clarity. *For being tough and strong and unafraid of the things that frighten me. For laughing because I'm not man enough to fight him.* He rose, brushing himself off absently. *Buck and the judge and Hollis. They laugh at me. But they don't know everything.*

He let himself into his front door as softly as any mouse. Mattie was asleep, her arm thrown across his empty space in the bed. Timm tiptoed to the tall oak wardrobe in the corner and found his gun behind the hanging clothes. The heavy gun was dusty, its bores corroded from standing a long time uncleaned, but that didn't matter. Timm was sure it would fire. He took the gun and a box of shells, glancing often at his sleeping wife as he slipped back to the hallway.

He reached the corner of the square in time to see Hollis mount the courthouse steps toward his office. A moment later, another figure loomed up unsteadily from the ground and staggered toward another entrance. Timm recognized Judge Blankenship.

No matter. Hollis and the judge might parade their dignity in public. Cy Timm had his dignity, too. He started toward the light that had appeared in the sheriff's window, then drew suddenly back. Crow was passing Parnell's store with his slow-footed, hopping gait, a long gun grasped in his bony hands. Timm faded into the shadows of the alley. His own gun and his resolve giving him comfort, he waited.

Judge Homer Blankenship dipped his handkerchief into a basin and pressed it against the side of his face. It came away bloody. *Hollis!* Hollis had walked away from him like a man who planned to live forever, leaving him — him, Homer Blankenship — to creep back to his chambers like a beaten dog. It was insufferable that a man of education and refinement should be abused by an arrogant barbarian like Hollis.

And now Hollis threatened more than his life. His reputation, his seat on the bench, the good name he planned to pass along to his children, everything important to him, was in jeopardy. Hollis couldn't strip him of office; it would never come to that. But even a breath of scandal could ruin his plans. Clearly, he had no time to waste.

Firm in his decision, Blankenship opened the closet door, moved aside a broom and mop, and drew out a shiny new Parker hammerless shotgun. No one knew about the gun, not even his wife. He had ordered it in secret for just such a contingency, and now was the time to act. A shame that his colleagues would be caught unprepared, but he had himself to think of. Hollis had to die at once, that very night.

Chapter 11

December 5, 1894

"Why, hell!" Castleberry's chin came up in an abrupt movement. He stepped back behind that narrow line in his soul. He studied King closely, finally nodding. "I should have seen that in you. Your build and your hair — but your eyes, mostly."

"I didn't know we favored. But Judge Blankenship seems to think so."

"Blankenship!" The rancher almost spat the word. "I'll thank you not to use his name under this roof."

"How about Buck Parnell's name? He seems to think you killed Hollis. Is that right?"

Castleberry's thin lips hinted a smile. "No special reason you should believe me. No special reason I should care," he said. "But this is the God's truth: I didn't kill him. If all I'd wanted was C.D. Hollis dead, I wouldn't've sneaked up on him in the night — nor used a shotgun, either."

"You're right," King said. "There's no special reason I should believe you." In his mind, though, the words rang true. Castleberry came from an old breed and a tough one. He'd be the kind to walk up and face his man — maybe with his vaqueros to flank him, but out in the open.

"Suit yourself," the rancher said with a dry chuckle. "But be a little careful about believing those vultures in town. They'd be right pleased to see me in my grave — pleased as they are to see C.D. in his."

"I'm told they hired him."

"Sure. To kill Donny — and maybe me, too."

The woman Socorro appeared at the bead curtain. "Lunch will soon be ready," she said.

Castleberry finished his coffee at a gulp and set the cup on the sideboard. Then he unstrapped his holster and took off the gunbelt. He hung the belt on the ten-point rack of the right-hand buck. "Let's go in to eat. We can get back to our talking afterward."

If Castleberry had anyone protecting his flank, King couldn't tell it. Having laid bare between them the ugliness and uncertainty of blood vengeance, the rancher had hung up his weapon in a show of truce. Jeff King couldn't tell whether this was the same man he'd met the day before. Whatever kind of lunacy it was, it certainly ran in the family.

Looking into his cup, King saw a sheepish face staring back at him, the face of a man overcome by local custom and lunacy that was catching. "Good enough," he said. He drank off the face in his cup and went to hang his gunbelt on the other rack of antlers. Freed from the weight of the gun, he turned to look again at Castleberry's parlor.

It wasn't like the house in Waxahachie where he'd been a boy, but he couldn't help feeling at home. He almost expected to see C.D. there.

"We'll look after each other, Jeff Davis. It's what brothers do."

"You're only half my brother."

King flinched. The vision faded. The far end of the room was empty. Beside the door stood a rack of shotguns and rifles. A short leg-of-mutton leather case leaned against the rack.

"What?"

"Your steak," Castleberry repeated. "Did you want it burned or raw, or someplace in between?"

Socorro was in the doorway, beaded strings draped across her shoulders. She watched King with bottomless dark eyes.

"Closer to raw," he said. What had they given him in the coffee?

"Hot brandy brings out the best in a man," Castleberry said. "Or maybe the worst." He grinned. "Sure don't do the memory no good, whichever it is."

Lunch was a bigger affair than King expected. He sat at the foot of a long table with Castleberry at its head. Saul and Octavio, the two vaqueros King had first seen in town, flanked the rancher left and right. When Octavio had first entered the dining room, he had stopped abruptly at the sight of King.

"I will not eat at the table with this man," he said in angry Spanish.

Saul glanced anxiously at Castleberry, then took the younger man's arm. "It is not for you to say. He is the guest of our patron."

"He has not shown the proper respect for the Miss Diana. He —" Octavio broke off, leaving that thought unfinished. He stood in the doorway, tall and proud, glaring at King but obviously unaware King understood his speech.

"Octavio," Castleberry said. He had seemed not to notice the quarrel. He gave the young man a thin smile and gestured to the chair on his left. "Sit here if you will." When Octavio hesitated, he added, "It is my wish."

"*Si, jefe.*" He had moved to the place Castleberry indicated, but the look he shot King showed he wasn't ready to forgive or forget.

Half a dozen other cowhands, older men most of them, filled the other places. They laughed and talked with Castleberry like old friends, but King felt the undercurrent of their respect for the rancher and their suspicion at his own presence.

"King." Castleberry leaned forward, and conversation along the table died. "Noel tells me that black of yours is *mucho caballo* — no mount for a couple of youngsters."

"I'd say Noel knows horseflesh."

"Beginning to. His grandfather's teaching him." Castleberry gestured down the table to the man seated at King's right. "Constanzo Alvarez. The best horse-gentler anybody ever saw, up until he tangled with a killer bronc. He's our farrier now."

King put out his hand. *"Con mucho gusto, señor."*

Alvarez was a small man, white of hair and mustache. His face was deeply wrinkled, but he held his back straight and met King's handshake with a firm, dry grip. "The black will do well," he said, his voice gentle, "with proper training. Much is in the training."

"Good enough for me," Castleberry said. "You of a mind to trade him?"

"I noticed a pair of colts down by the corral," King answered. "What value would you put on them?"

"Those little sorrels? Twins. That don't happen one time in a hundred. Killed their mother." The rancher rubbed his chin. "Well, they're just underfoot now. Was you minded to trade, I suppose —"

Alvarez interrupted with a sharp burst of Spanish. King frowned slightly to suggest puzzlement. He saw no need to show Castleberry and the others that he understood. *"Never show your cards till the hand's over,"* C.D. used to say. *"And don't show them then unless you have to."*

"Constanzo thinks I'm about to cheat you," the rancher said. "Tell you what. We'll trade the colts for your black and his saddle, and Constanzo will make you saddles for the both of them to fit the Hollis boys."

"Done."

"All right!" Castleberry said. "Socorro! Let's see that cake that you've been working on."

When the others had gone back to work, Castleberry turned to King. "Come upstairs with me for a minute," he said. "Emma would like to meet you."

King followed him up the broad stairway and along a spacious hall to a door near the end of the corridor. There the rancher paused and knocked.

"Emma? Are you awake? I'm bringing our company."

Without waiting for an answer, he opened the door and stepped softly inside, motioning King to follow. King had expected the room to be dark, but light flowed into it through the wide, uncurtained window. Emma Castleberry lay like a frail gray shadow in the massive four-poster bed.

Her bloodless hands were crossed on the coverlet and her thin body lay motionless, face turned to the window.

"Emma," Castleberry said again. "I've brought you some company."

Slowly, the gray head turned toward them. King felt a shock as she looked at him with deep, luminous brown eyes. For a moment, her eyes seemed the only living thing about her. Then her pale lips lifted in the ghost of a smile and she moved to sit up in the bed.

"Why, hello, young man," she said softly. "I

was just watching the clouds. There's like to be a norther soon."

"Yes ma'am."

Castleberry crossed to the bed and touched her hair. It was white, carefully combed and pulled back into a braid. The braided hair, the snowy white sheets on the bed, the spotless cleanliness of the room, all spoke of devoted care.

"Emma, this is Jeff King," the rancher said. He looked at King. "Emma's tired, but I knew she'd want to meet you. We'll just say good day and go along."

"No," Emma Castleberry said in her soft whisper. She paused and seemed to rest a moment. "Please sit down. It's so good to see someone young again."

"Thank you, ma'am." King came forward to a ladderback chair near the bedside. "It's kind of you to have me here."

Emma Castleberry had questions which she asked in a hushed, eager voice. *What had brought him here?* A horse trade. She didn't think so. *Isn't it to see my daughter?* Well, partly, Ma'am. *Of course it was. But where did he hail from?* Waxahachie. *Had he come to see some of his people?* Yes. *What was his line of work?*

King hesitated just a heartbeat. Then he looked past the woman to her husband. "I'm a Texas Ranger," he said.

Castleberry smiled ever so slightly, but did not look at King. Throughout their talk, he had sat on the edge of the bed and looked at his wife.

114

Now he touched her hand and stood. "I know you're tired, Emma. Best we go along."

"But I haven't finished my talk with Mr. King."

King cleared his throat. "I'll have to be going, ma'am. But I promise I'll come back to finish our visit."

"All right then. It was nice to meet you, young man."

"My pleasure, ma'am."

Downstairs in the parlor, Castleberry stood with his back to the fire and watched King. "You lied to me."

"No."

"Saul said you were a Ranger. He's seldom wrong about a man."

"I never denied I was a Ranger, just that I'd been sent. When we talked, I hadn't."

"Now you have?"

"That's right."

Castleberry nodded slowly. "I see. I just didn't ask the right question." He put his hands behind him, reaching out to the fire. He seemed older, grayer. "Still figure me for the one, do you?"

"You own a shotgun."

Castleberry gave a gray laugh. "Five — no, six now, not counting Diana's. She's a better wing shot than I am — you'll have to hunt with us sometime. Everybody owns a shotgun."

"I don't."

"You can use one of mine."

"He killed your son."

The rancher's thin lips tightened and his hands jerked into clenched fists. "Hollis pulled the trigger. That damned town killed my son — the town and them that run it."

"How?"

"They want my ranch." Castleberry's face and voice showed his anger, a live ember in gray ashes. "They got half of it already — stole it, rather. All the land north of the gate you come in at, clear north to the Pecos. They stole it, and they're selling it off to pilgrims coming in to fence the country."

"Wasn't that open range?"

The rancher glared at him. "Open range, hell! I run my cattle there thirty years, back before there was anything here but me and the Army and the Apaches. What does it take to make something yours? There's no honor in a man that covets his neighbor's ox or ass or maidservant — nor his land, either."

King didn't answer. He knew the story well enough. He'd heard plenty of others like it. Someone who knew law and surveying had staked the waterholes, claimed them, bought and fenced them. Without water, Castleberry couldn't run his cattle on that wide land any longer. Without water, he couldn't live.

"I didn't see what they were doing at first," Castleberry said as if he'd overheard King's thought. "Then I tried to do some claiming of my own, in my name and my vaqueros, but my messages to Austin didn't get through. I saved

116

what I could." He stopped, then said, "Donny meant to get back the rest. So they brought C.D. in to kill him."

"C.D. wasn't a hired killer."

"Wasn't he? How close did you keep company with him the last few years?"

King didn't answer. After a moment, the rancher shook his head.

"Likely he wasn't," he said at last. "Likely he didn't know what was at the bottom of it all. My guess is that he found out afterward, and they had to kill him."

"So you think they were behind it, the judge and his bunch?"

"Since I didn't kill him, it figures them in town did. If he was onto them, he'd have told them so. Your brother was damned direct."

"Like you?"

"Like you. Take a lesson."

"Haven't got the time."

"Take some help, then."

"Help?" King didn't try to hide his surprise. "From you?"

Castleberry laughed. "Had a lot of other offers, have you?"

"Well, not so many," King admitted. "First part's going to be hard, though. I want to know everything that happened between C.D. and your boy."

Chapter 12

November 19, 1894

C.D. Hollis locked his office door and stood listening. Nothing stirred in the room or in the night outside. Satisfied, he lit the kerosene lamp. Locking the door was only a gesture. Blankenship had bled the county dry of tax money, but his pretty courthouse was still unfinished, without shutters or shades. Anyone who felt like it could look straight through the uncurtained windows.

Hell, let 'em come! Hollis thought. He was tired — tired physically, but even more weary of the cat-and-mouse struggle with Blankenship and Castleberry. Sinking into his office chair, he took a bottle from the lower drawer of his desk.

It gets so's it's not fun anymore, Jeff Davis. Guess I should've taught you that, excepting I'm only learning it myself.

He drank, then rolled back the desktop and found his leatherbound notebook. A lot was happening, and he didn't want to forget anything when the time came to tell Jeff. He could see his way open now; no time to slip up. He hoped Jeff would come soon — tomorrow, maybe. Cuervo was a good man when he wasn't drinking, but that wasn't often.

Sheriff C.D. Hollis had been writing for almost ten minutes when something touched the glass of the window behind him with a tiny, audible clink. He reacted instantly, dropping his silver fountain pen and snatching for his Colt. The clink was followed by a shattering roar. The window sleeted inward, spraying Hollis with chunks of glass, but the core of the charge went into the wall over his head. He slid from the chair onto one knee and began to turn, pistol cocked in his hand. His mind marveled that anyone could miss with a shotgun at twelve feet, while his body, acting independently on old instinct, moved to kill his attacker.

His finger was closing on the trigger when smoke and flame reached out to touch his chest. The impact of the bunched lead shot flung him back across the desk and off onto the floor again. He was already dead when the Colt in his hand roared, driving a heavy slug into the new hardwood paneling beside the window.

Chapter 13

December 5, 1894

Jeff King made his excuses rather than stay for supper at the DC, but the early December twilight had come on before he left. Riding back toward Willow Springs in the cold light of a sickle moon, he sorted out his reasons. Try as he might, he couldn't help liking the Castleberrys — all three of them. He felt comfortable at the ranch. It reminded him of the home he'd known too briefly as a child.

For a moment, two coffins gleamed white in the moonlight. He remembered tears, grief, anger, a miserable sense of loss — and C. D. Hollis, who had come home from no one knew where for the funeral. C.D., who was as good as his promise, who was always there when he was needed.

"I came back too late, Jeff Davis." King remembered the words now. They hadn't meant anything much to him at the time. *"I wish to God I'd had a chance to talk to them before — well, no matter."* Then or later, it was the only time he'd ever heard C.D. voice a regret. *"Hard lines, Jeff. We'll have to look after each other now, and both*

of us after Nancy. That's what brothers do."

"That's what brothers do," King repeated softly, and knew his reason for leaving the DC. There he was too trusting, too ready to believe what people told him. No matter what Castleberry said, King couldn't afford to forget the rancher had the best reason he'd seen so far for wanting C.D. dead.

Diana. The thought of her came with the force of a physical presence. She hadn't returned from town, and he'd more than half expected to meet her on the road. He wondered where she'd gone and why no one at the ranch had seemed concerned about her. If they had met, he might have changed his mind and ridden back with her to the DC. But the road and the range were empty except for two shadowy riders at the edge of his vision, escorting him back to the Castleberry gate. He closed the gate and they dropped away, leaving him to ride the last half mile alone.

Full darkness had come by the time he reached town, but there was still life and light at the two saloons along the square. Snatches of loud talk and music drifted down to the deserted livery stable. King tended the roan himself and left a dollar at the front desk. Clear and strong from one of the saloons, a man's voice lifted above the throb of a guitar in an old Mexican ballad.

Absently whistling along, King rested his carbine lightly over his shoulder and pushed open one of the big wooden doors. He stepped through

121

into the cold, clean night wind.

Flame lanced from the darkness between two buildings. A deep, reverberating *boom!* came an instant later. The door smashed against King and splinters showered his head and shoulders. He stumbled and went to one knee, almost dropping the carbine. Then he had it in both hands, working the lever as he brought it to bear on the place the shot had come from. Still half blinded by the muzzle flash, he strained eyes and ears to find a target.

"Hey! What the hell!"

Music and talk from the saloons had died in an instant. Now a dozen or more men came pouring through the lighted doorways onto the square.

"It's him! What's 'is name — King!"

"Hollis's brother!"

"Who'd he shoot?"

"Who shot him, more likely!"

King gave up. He'd seen no movement, and any sound would have been lost like a grain of sand in the desert. He couldn't just start shooting. Lowering the carbine's hammer, he stood up just as the first of the saloon crowd reached him.

"Hey, mister, you all right? What happened? Whoooeee! Look at that door."

King looked. The planks a foot or two above his head had vanished into a ragged hole the size of a bucket. "Shotgun," he said. "Somebody took a shot at me." He raised his voice. "From over by the alley. Did anybody see who it was? Or where he went?"

"Not me. We was most of us in the Lost Mule."

A murmur of agreement came from the group that had gathered around King. He searched their faces but found nobody he recognized. "Somebody said I was Hollis's brother. Who was that?"

For a minute, they all looked at each other without speaking. Then a lean brown man in overalls took a reluctant step out.

"Well. Me, I guess," he said. "Ain't you — meaning no offense?"

"None taken. And I am. But who told you?"

"Well. I don't rightly remember who. Seems like we alls knowed it. It's around town — that you's Hollis's kin."

"And damn near ended up like him, too," a burly man laughed. "That door looks like the sheriff's office, 'cepting without the blood!"

King swung his head and the carbine's muzzle around the big man's way. "Can't say I think that's funny," he said softly.

The man bristled and balled his fists. His eyes were bloodshot and his voice slurred. "That's 'cause you don't know what a bastard Hollis was!" He laughed again. "You should've seen it. Busted glass and blood all over, and Hollis —"

King swung the Winchester in a short, savage arc. Its stock clipped the speaker's jaw with a sobering crack and he dropped in midsentence.

Silence fell, sudden and complete. Nobody moved to help him, but the faces that stared at King were surprised and hostile. He stepped back against the doors, the carbine across his chest.

"Now that I have your attention, I want the man who shot at me. Some of you might know who it was. If you feel like telling, I won't be hard to find."

"Well." The man in the overalls hadn't been intimidated. "What's you figure to do with him? Bust his jaw, too? Or shoot him down?"

"Arrest him." King hesitated, but there wasn't much profit left in hiding anything. He took the circled star from his pocket and pinned it to his shirt. "I'm a Texas Ranger."

"Be damned! What'd I tell you!" somebody said. An excited babble broke out, and then Judge Blankenship's deep voice overrode it.

"Gentlemen, gentlemen! Why this commotion?" The judge had stopped behind the crowd. "Can someone tell me what's happened?"

"Some poor fool took a shot at the Ranger!"

"Some poor shot, you mean. Look at that hole."

King glanced up, surprised. He hadn't had time to think about it, but the shot had gone awfully high. Maybe something had startled the man with the shotgun. But maybe the shot hadn't been meant to kill him.

Buck Parnell came trotting from the direction of the courthouse. "All right, break it up." He gestured with the barrel of the long gun he carried. "Move along. We're going to get some peace and quiet if I have to arrest every drunk —"

He stopped abruptly when he saw King and the judge. A few of the crowd whistled and clapped, but most of them began finding business somewhere else. In a few moments, the street was almost deserted again.

"Fired that gun lately, have you?" King asked.

Buck looked at him, then at the hole in the door. He grinned. "Not tonight, friend. And I wouldn't have missed." He hefted the gun. "Hell, this ain't even a shotgun, see."

He hefted the gun. In the light King recognized it as an old pump-action Colt rifle.

"Does the county own a shotgun?"

"Sure. Back at my office."

"Mind if I look at it?"

"Damn right!"

King moved forward, and Blankenship stepped between him and Buck. *Seems he's always doing that,* King thought. *Don't know if I should thank him or not.*

"Hold," the judge said in his courtroom voice. "Gentlemen, you're both lawmen." He looked meaningfully at King's badge. "Let's not stand and point guns at one another. Mr. King, if you'll lower your rifle, I think Buck will be reasonable."

Looking past Blankenship, Buck handed the judge his rifle. King didn't understand until he noticed the three men still remaining in the street. Two of them were Eli Parnell and Cy

125

Timm. Both held shotguns as if they had some idea what they were for. The third man, similarly armed but looking more confident, was the station agent, Henry Drumm.

"Fair enough," King said. His carbine against the four of them didn't strike him as a worthwhile test of justice. He lowered the Winchester's hammer to safe and let the muzzle point at the ground. "Would it do any good to ask if any of these other guns were fired tonight?"

The three looked at Blankenship, and some signal seemed to pass among them. Drumm stepped forward first, breaking open his Greener. "Suit yourself, mister. Me, I just came along to keep the peace. We're right touchy about gunfire since —" he hesitated, then shrugged — "since your brother was killed."

"All right." King spread his hands in an unconscious gesture of defeat. If they were willing to let him look, it wasn't likely he'd learn anything. "I don't suppose it was you that mentioned to these folks that I was a Ranger? None of you seemed too surprised, and that telegram I sent was about the only hint I gave out."

"Damn right he mentioned it, and a good thing," Buck Parnell put in. "Listen, friend, I ain't been a lawman very long, but you got no business stirring up trouble in my town without telling me. You like to've had us shooting at each other."

King started to answer, then bit back words and anger. There was some justice in what Buck

126

said, much as he hated to admit it.

"I must agree," Blankenship said. "Your late brother had the same habit of concealing his badge. I'm afraid it did not serve him well."

"Less of a target, when there's skunks that might shoot you from ambush," King said. He turned to Buck. "I guess you'll look for whoever did this as hard as you've looked for C.D.'s killer?"

"You bet," Buck said.

Blankenship cleared his throat. "I do not miss the irony in your words, Ranger," he said. "Please believe we mean you no harm. Now that we know who you really are, we will help your efforts in any way we can — including finding the person who tried to kill you."

"I doubt I'll be able to sleep until I hear from you," King muttered. His face and neck were beginning to hurt. He'd picked up a few splinters, if not some stray pellets from the shotgun's charge. He'd also had plenty of the judge and his cronies for one night — all except one of them, maybe. "Tell you what, how about one of you walking me to the Hollis house — just to be sure I get there safe."

Buck barked a laugh. "Sure! And hold your hand, too."

"All of us, if you like," Blankenship said.

"No." King grinned, and that hurt too. "No, I'd like Mr. Timm to come along. He strikes me as the most trustworthy of the lot of you."

"Me?" Cy Timm's anguished squeak matched

the sudden twitch of his shoulders. "No! I mean, why — ?"

"An excellent choice," Blankenship cut in smoothly. "Go along, Cy. It'll be quite all right."

"But —" Timm began again. Then he stopped and gripped his shotgun hard with both hands. "Well — all right."

King stepped away from the wall and Timm hesitantly fell in beside him. Together, they crossed the street and started along the edge of the square.

"What the hell," Buck said, scratching his unruly red hair. "Why's King want a mouse along? It don't add up."

"It adds," Drumm said softly. Blankenship shot him a sharp look.

"What's that?"

"Nothing, Judge. Nothing important."

Cy Timm scurried along at King's side, twisting his head frantically as he tried to watch every alley and doorway. "Listen," he panted, "Surely he won't take another shot at you tonight! Surely not! Do you think he will?"

"Not while he's where I can watch him," King said. "Keep a step in front of me."

"What? Watch who?" Timm stopped from pure astonishment. "You think *I* shot at you?"

"The bunch of you remind me of a doctored poker hand — five deuces. Why shouldn't it be you?"

He gave Timm a shove that set him into motion again. The smaller man fairly skipped along to keep pace with King's long stride, his voice an indignant squeak.

"Why in thunder would I want to shoot at you — or at anybody? I tell you, I haven't fired this old gun since eighty-seven or eighty-eight, and you can see that for yourself!"

King swung away from the square, pulling Timm with him onto the rutted path that led to the Hollis place. "Maybe you'd better practice, then," he said. "You're apt to need protection if you keep dabbling in murder — and if you keep writing letters."

Timm had been stumbling manfully along the dark pathway. At that, he stopped again, so abruptly that King almost fell over him.

"Letters? What letters? I don't know —"

"Probably you don't know about beans, either. Probably you've never gambled for a man's life with a handful, nor drawn a black bean for yourself."

"How — ?" Timm's knees buckled and he almost fell. With a shudder, he pulled himself erect again and stared at King. "I don't know," he said. "I don't know what you mean."

"Good thing. Else I might wonder if you didn't put a load of shot into my brother."

Timm shuddered and turned away, plunging like a hare up the trail. Now it was King who had to hurry to keep up.

"I didn't!" Timm squeaked. "I never! I've

never killed anybody, nor want to. Why are you saying these things?"

"You laid it out pretty plain in your letter. You drew the black bean, but somebody else beat you off the mark."

Timm stared at him with a mixture of fear and puzzlement. "What? I don't know what letter you're talking about." He frowned, twitching his mouth like a mouse worrying a grain of corn. "You're trying to trip me up," he said. "Trying to make me say something that — that I don't mean. Just like your brother, that's what you are!"

"Just like him," King agreed grimly. "Calm and quiet and gentle until I find out a man's lying to me. Right now you're about one mouse step from the edge of my patience and my temper both."

"I don't know what you mean."

"Keep walking. You wrote the Adjutant General a letter. Said you'd testify in return for amnesty." King rode over Timm's squeak of protest. "Don't lie. You're the only one it could have been. I'm offering the amnesty, but you'd better talk while your friends aren't around to hear. Right now."

"No!"

Timm turned suddenly, the muzzles of the shotgun swinging upward. King didn't wait to see if the move was accidental or intentional. He stepped in fast, grabbing for the gunbarrels with his free hand while he brought the hand holding the carbine up to knock the smaller man aside. Timm staggered backward, and King twisted the shotgun out of his hands.

"God of Mighty!" Timm staggered back against the railing of the Hollis porch, his eyes wide with surprise and fear. "Do you mean to kill me?"

King looked down at Timm's old shotgun. There were streaks of rust around the breech that showed it hadn't been opened for a long time. The big mule-eared hammers weren't cocked for firing.

"Hell," King said tiredly. With a sudden, violent motion, he swung the gun up as if it were an axe and smashed it into the ground. The wooden stock shattered and broke free, and King slung the barrels off into the darkness.

Still staring at him, Timm pulled himself away from the railing. "God's my witness, King," he said. "I don't know anything about that letter. If there is such a thing, I didn't send it." He paused, then straightened defiantly. "And it's a pack of lies, all the same. Just you prove it's not!"

"Maybe you don't know about the letter," King said. "But you know about the beans, and you know more about C.D.'s murder than you're letting on. I gave you your chance to turn evidence and live. If you've decided to die with your friends, that's your right."

Timm started to speak, but his voice came out a squeak. He pressed his lips together and tried again. "Hollis used to talk that way," he said.

Red anger burned through King, washing away his pain and weariness. "Get away from here," he grated. He swung up the carbine. "Get away. Else God's my witness, I'll shoot you where you stand."

Timm started to speak again, thought better of it, and darted away down the trail. King watched until he'd scurried out of sight in the darkness, then turned to mount the steps to the porch. His anger was draining away. He was tired. His shirt was stiff from dried blood and his neck and shoulders hurt. Worst, he had the nagging feeling he might be making a fool of himself.

Suppose Timm was telling the truth. Suppose he didn't know about the letter. Then what?

The brown dog rose from a corner of the porch and came to him, whining anxiously. King bent to rub the shaggy head.

"Hungry? All right, I'll get you some grub. Just hold your horses."

Straightening, he opened the screen and reached for the doorknob. The door was locked.

Immediately, King stepped aside, away from the doorway, bringing the carbine down and thumbing back the hammer. The sense that he'd made a fool of himself returned, sharper now. While he'd wasted time with Timm, any one of the others — or all of them, for that matter — could have hurried ahead to meet him. Cautiously, keeping his body well away from the door, he stretched out an arm and jiggled the doorknob, more loudly this time. Someone moved inside the house and King waited for a charge of buckshot to come through the door. Instead, he heard the soft cry of a nighthawk.

"Jeff?" it sang softly. "Jeff, is that you?"

Chapter 14

November 19, 1894

With a lack of dignity he would ordinarily have considered unseemly, Homer Blankenship dashed up the stairs and fumbled desperately with the locked door of his chambers. When he finally managed to get inside, he closed the door as softly as his frantic haste would allow and flung himself across the room to the closet. He tossed the shotgun deep into its recesses, careless of the fine finish of the stock, then slammed and locked the door. Panting, he stared up at the skylight while he fought the panic that gripped his mind.

Gradually his breathing slowed and he mastered himself. Brushing the dust from his coat, he stood erect. Then he drew a small revolver from the pocket of his coat and strode unhurriedly back to the stairs that led down to the sheriff's office. As the first person on the scene, Judge Homer Blankenship had discovered the body of Sheriff C.D. Hollis, slain by person or persons unknown.

Hopping awkwardly up the stone steps with his shotgun in his hands, cursing in two languages, Crow was the second man to reach the door of the sheriff's office. He found Judge Blankenship in the doorway, staring whitefaced at the scene inside.

"Por Dios," Crow moaned and broke into a fit of coughing. The judge turned on him, glaring, the small pistol ready.

"What's this?" he demanded. "What are you doing with that gun? Are you responsible for this?"

"Oh, God," Crow said without understanding. "Must be I am. Should've been on watch, where's he'd set me. Where is he? Where's the sheriff, caw-haw?"

For answer, Blankenship stood aside and let Crow shove into the office. He got a step further than the judge had, then stopped with a helpless growl deep in his throat. Broken and on its side, a chair lay beneath the shattered window. Bits of paper covered with writing were scattered on the floor as if a whirlwind had swept through the room, and slivers of glass sparkled and crunched underfoot like snowflakes. Above the desk a torn and pockmarked section of the paneled wall had been newly painted red.

C.D. Hollis lay sprawled on his back, one booted foot resting on the desktop, the fingers of one hand still locked around his heavy Colt revolver. His hat had fallen across his face. The tatters of his vest and once-white shirt glistened with the same dark wet redness as the wall. The boot on the desk gleamed with polish, but its sole was ringed and thin with circles of wear. Crow understood that.

"What are you doing here?" Blankenship demanded again. "Speak up, if you don't want to be charged with murder."

"Caw!" Crow's sudden hack could have been either a cough or a laugh. "Blame me for this, would you? Not Cuervo. Not old stupid Crow what ain't got good sense, caw-haw!" He stared at Blankenship with round, white-rimmed eyes until the judge looked away. "Just passing by, I was, and heard the racket, and still got both loads in this old gun, more's the pity."

"But you're here — and with the appropriate weapon."

Crow inspected the shotgun as if he'd never see one before. "Sure enough. And might be's there's others carrying shotguns around tonight." He stood the gun against the wall. "Might be's I'd tell who else I saw, did somebody ask me, caw-caw-caw-haw!"

"Be quiet, you — !"

Blankenship broke off. Others were coming, their voices loud and questioning, their boot heels ringing on the marble steps. The judge turned to meet them. Crow stepped softly into the sheriff's office and closed the door behind him.

The floor reminded him of the layers of fool's gold he'd seen once in a cave by the Rio Grande. A breeze from the broken window swayed the hanging lamp so light moved and shimmered on the shards of glass. Watching the light, Crow went to the corner to get his broom and began to sweep glass, papers, and bits of shattered windowframe into a pile in the center of the room. From the commotion outside, he could pick out individual voices.

"What's he doing in there?"

"Did he do the killing?"

"My God, Judge, are you sick? You look like *you* did it."

"Guard your tongue! I — I discovered the — sheriff. I was in my chambers —"

Crow went on sweeping. He heard their voices, knew the names of the first ones to come, ignored them all.

"Cy, what's wrong with you? Get away from here with that shotgun!"

"Listen, I want to know what that crazy old buzzard is doing in there!"

"I heard you. We all did. I believe he is sweeping."

"Sweeping? That's —"

"Crazy? Perhaps. Henry, please be so good as to fetch Mr. Felder. He can take — Sheriff Hollis — away."

"I don't think we better do that. Somebody needs to look into this — to investigate."

"Buck's right, Judge. Moving — him — might look funny. We need a proper investigation."

"It will look considerably better than leaving him where he is. I shall appoint a temporary sheriff to look into the killing. I believe —"

"Judge, Eli, listen. The whole town's coming. This ain't no time for a meeting."

"Agreed. I'll handle this. Come on."

Crow listened and knew his own truths and kept sweeping. He avoided the clots and spatters of blood that would stick to his broom. He could scrape them up when they hardened. Then the door opened and Judge Blankenship came in, followed by Buck and Eli Parnell. Several more men clustered at the office door, peering inside. Crow leaned on his broom and admired the pile of glass and papers that had accumulated.

"God's grace!" Buck murmured. "I didn't know it would look like this."

Blankenship's courtroom voice drowned him out. "Please keep back, gentlemen. Mr. Felder will be here soon. I'm deputizing Buck Parnell to act as sheriff until an election can be held."

"Well," a man in overalls said. "Guess that's all right, you being the judge and all. But we want to know what's happened here."

Two or three in the crowd behind him made sounds of assent. Blankenship nodded gravely.

"As do we all gentlemen. Buck will get to the bottom of this terrible crime."

"And the fox'll guard the henhouse," Crow muttered, losing the words in a bout of coughing.

Blankenship glanced at him, then went on. "Now, if you'll all clear away, our new sheriff and I will examine the evidence. Eli, please escort these good citizens downstairs."

With some help from Henry Drumm, Eli got

the crowd herded outside. Crow leaned on his broom while Buck and the judge looked again at the wrecked office and the dead man who'd worked there.

"Where's his gun?"

"In his hand." Buck hesitated, then went to get it. "Fired twice," he said. He put the pistol carefully on the desk and wiped his hands. "Everything in here's bloody."

"And the shotgun was fired twice also."

Blankenship gestured at the splintered patch near the ceiling, then at the broad red spray on the wall. In its center, a mangled disc of metal hung nailed like a painting.

"Lord God," Buck muttered. "That was his badge. I never would've thought what a shotgun can do to a man." He shook himself and looked at Blankenship, his voice subdued. "Question is, which of us did it? And how can we put it off on Castleberry?"

"Hush!" Blankenship glanced quickly at Crow. The little man was staring vacantly at Hollis's body, seemingly unaware of the others. "Ah, here's Mr. Felder. We'll let him deal with our late friend while we talk elsewhere. Come along — Sheriff."

Crow leaned on his broom while the undertaker and his assistant, talking and gesturing between themselves, loaded the sheriff on a little cart and took him away. Buck had been right; there was blood everywhere. Crow straightened the desk, found more blood and glass behind it,

139

and put his broom aside. He was going to need a mop. And water. A lot of water.

By the time he had the office in tolerable shape again, the night was well along and things were quiet. Crow took a last look around. His dark eye fell on the desktop, still marred with a stain no scrubbing could remove. Felder had left the sheriff's gun. Near it, shoved back beneath the pigeonholes, was a brown leather notebook and a shiny fountain pen.

"Well, now," Crow chirped happily. Crossing the room, he tucked the gun into his waistband and slipped the other items into his pocket. A more thoughtful man might have taken them as pay for a dirty job, but that never occurred to Cuervo. He liked shiny things, and that was enough.

Chapter 15

December 5, 1894

A key rattled in the lock and the door opened slowly, just a crack. Half hidden by a lock of fox-red hair, a blue eye peered out at King.

"Jeff, I —" Sheila Parnell began.

Her voice cut off in a startled squeal when King hit the door, shoving it back with his shoulder and pushing inside. Before she could recover from her surprise, he grabbed her slender arm and pushed her ahead of him into the dimly lit parlor.

"Jeff!" she cried, but King held her until he was sure the parlor was empty. Then he bolted the door and steered her through the rest of the house, one dark room after the other. When he was certain they were alone, he drew her back to the parlor and laid the carbine aside.

"Jeff!" The bird cry was puzzled, fearful. "What — why did you do that? You hurt me!"

He turned up the lamp and looked at her. She stared forlornly downward, not looking at him, her eyes brimming with tears. Like a hurt child, she raised a white hand to touch his fingers where they gripped her upper arm.

"Please," she said.

"Who came with you?"

"Nobody."

"Who sent you?"

"No — no one. Nobody even knows I'm here. I thought — I thought you'd be glad to see me. What's wrong with you?"

She turned round into him without trying to free her arm. The soft warmth of her breasts nestled against his chest. When she tilted her face up to look into his eyes, the dizzying scent of heliotrope rose into his nostrils. Her free hand brushed his cheek as lightly as a butterfly's wing — and then she pulled back suddenly, staring wide-eyed at the blood on her fingers.

"That's what's wrong with me," King said grimly. "Somebody fired his shotgun my way. Chances are it was somebody you know."

"No — no, he wouldn't!" She caught herself. "I mean, I don't know who —"

"I know what you mean."

He thrust her away, releasing her arm at last. Her long coat lay on the sofa and he picked it up, running his hands over it swiftly. Satisfied it held no weapon, he tossed it aside. He was fairly certain nothing was hidden in the dress that clung so faithfully to her body. Turning away from her, he eased the bloodstained jacket off his shoulders.

"Here," Sheila Parnell said. "Let me help you."

Her voice still held a faint tremble. She drew

the sleeves off his arms and let the coat fall to the floor. When he turned toward her, she took a lacy handkerchief from the bosom of her dress and softly touched it to the cuts on the side of his face. King caught her wrist and she looked boldly into his eyes. When he'd first seen her on the train, she'd been acting the part of a tease, offering much less than her words suggested. Now her silence was full of hidden promise. ✑

Slowly, she drew her hand out of his grasp, reaching up to remove his hat. "I could reach your face better if you sat down," she said.

King didn't move. After a moment, Sheila moved to him, slid her slender arms around his neck. Gently, she pulled his face down to her level and kissed him.

King thought of several reasons he should push her away, but none of them seemed pressing. They hung at the edge of his mind like vague stars, cold and distant compared to the immediacy of her embrace. As her arms tightened and she nestled more closely into him, he knew how a bird felt caught in midair by a falcon.

When finally she moved her mouth away, she whispered, "No. I don't know anyone who would shoot at you."

He watched her lips as she spoke, drawn to them. "You ought to get out more," he said. "Meet people."

The full lips curled into a smile. She leaned nearer again, but King put his hands on her shoulders.

"Failing that, you might get to know your husband a little better."

Her smile vanished. She took a step back, wary and frightened.

"Or your brother-in-law."

He might as well have struck her. Her cheeks flamed and she caught back a sob in her throat. "No!" she cried. She pressed the bloody handkerchief to her eyes. "No, you don't know them. Eli would never hurt anyone — surely not a lawman!"

"And Buck?"

"He wouldn't!" She cried harder, shook her head more fiercely. "He's not like that. He flares up, but he'd never really — shoot — anyone."

"Then he's surely gone into the wrong business."

"But it's true! Why won't you believe me? Why won't you believe he's — they're — innocent?"

"Buck hasn't acted very innocent."

"Well, what do you expect, with you acting like you think he did it every minute?" She came to him again, snuggling to his chest. Her lips touched the side of his neck. "Jeff, please believe me. They didn't have any reason to hurt your brother. Nobody did . . ." She kissed his neck softly. ". . . except Castleberry."

"It means this much to you, does it?"

"You have to believe me. I'll do anything. I'll go with you, tonight, anywhere you say. Or — I'll stay with you here."

"If I'll leave Buck out of it."

"Yes!" The word burst out. Then she caught herself. "Eli and Buck. Both of them." She pulled King's face around until their lips touched again. "I can testify they had nothing to do with it."

King breathed deeply of heliotrope and the warm scent that belonged to Sheila. "Can you?" he murmured.

"I was with — them. Both of them. When it happened. We were in the kitchen, playing dominoes. I remember, because we heard the shots and Eli and Buck ran to see what the matter was."

"Leaving you alone in the house?"

"Of course." She tried another smile. "I wasn't afraid. I'm braver than you think."

"Did you have the window open?"

"Y— no! It was cold outside."

"But you heard shots anyway, from clear down at the courthouse?"

She stepped back and stared at him defiantly. "Yes," she said. Under his steady gaze, her eyes wavered and filled with tears. She lowered her head and sobbed into the handkerchief. "Well, it's true. Please believe me. I meant what I said. I'll do anything you want."

Any man's heart would go out to her, King thought. Aloud, he said, "I'm trying to figure out . . ."

"Yes?" Sheila looked up at him, eager, dry-eyed, fetching.

". . . what you want me to do."

"But . . ."

"Do you want me to take you up on your offer? Or had you rather I'd go kill Castleberry and let his vaqueros kill me so all of you will be free to finish taking his ranch?"

"His ranch?" For a moment, her pale face drew into a puzzled frown. "I don't know what you mean."

King believed her. "Never mind," he said.

"But I wish you'd take me away from here. Let's go tonight, on the late train, anywhere — wherever you say."

"That's what you want most, is it? To get me out of town?"

"I don't want Buck killed," she said softly. "Nor Eli. I want you to believe they didn't have anything to do with your brother's killing. That's what I want the worst."

She began to cry again, not theatrically this time, but with harsh, desperate sobs that shook her fragile shoulders.

King reached out and carefully folded her into his arms.

"I think there's something you want more than that," he said. "I think you wish you could believe that yourself."

King took some time getting Sheila Parnell into her coat and ready to go home. Her eyes were puffy and red from tears and her hair was mussed, but even making those allowances King had to admit she was still a beautiful woman. She was silent as he took up the carbine again and unlocked the door for her. Then she put her hand on his arm and looked up into his eyes.

"Please, Jeff," she whispered. "Don't think bad of me. I just don't want you to make a mistake."

He couldn't tell if she meant it or not, but it didn't matter. "I may make more than one," he said. "But I'll still end up where I'm going." He swung the door open for her. "Good night, Mrs. Parnell."

She pressed her lips together and turned away, stepping out onto the porch. Then she gave a start and a queer little bird cry of surprise. Frozen in the act of coming up the steps, Diana Castleberry stared first at her and then at King in the doorway. The brown and white dog frolicked unnoticed around her feet. Sheila recovered first and gave King a dazzling smile.

"Good night, Jeff," she said. "And thank you ever so much. I hope I'll see you again soon."

She brushed past Diana and walked quickly away into the darkness, her head high. Diana turned to watch her, then looked back at King, her face white in the soft light from the doorway.

"You," she said.

King sighed. There was no point in explaining anything, and no hope for the hot water and rest his aching body craved much more than it craved a visit from Diana Castleberry just then.

"You might as well come in," he told her. "Unless you think it will damage your reputation." He looked at the dog and shook his head. "Hell of a watchdog you are."

Diana's eyes narrowed, but her expression was still unreadable. She wore the long black riding habit King had seen before, and her raven hair was braided into a tight crown around her temples. She looked at him a moment longer, then came stiffly up the steps and into the parlor. She stopped there, her hands on her hips, fire in her nightdark eyes.

"You," she said again. "With her. What do you think you're doing?"

King closed and bolted the door, then laid the Winchester aside. "Right now, I'm getting ready to feed my dog," he said. "It'll just take a minute."

He went into the kitchen and found the scraps he'd set aside for the dog. He was taking an egg from the cupboard when he heard Diana's steps behind him. He turned toward her.

"What — ?"

She slapped him, a swift, backhand blow the way her father would have struck it, hard enough to snap his teeth together and right across the damage done by the splinters. He gave ground, bumping backward against the cabinet as she drew back her hand for another blow.

King caught it halfway between them, but he didn't have time to put the egg down. It splattered over both of them, spraying white and yellow flecks over her face and hair. She tossed her head and swung with her other hand. King blocked with the edge of his hand, chopping across her wrist hard enough to wring a gasp of pain from her. Before she could try again, he'd pinioned both wrists with his hands.

"If you kick, I'll break your arm," he said.

She glared. He didn't know if she believed him, but she didn't kick. "I told you to wait at the ranch until I came back!" she snapped.

"I waited until dark and you didn't come. Then I had other business to attend to."

"Yes, I saw that other business." She tried to pull free of his grip. "First you come back to get shot at, and then I come to help you and find you with that redhaired trollop! Let me go!"

"Do you promise to behave?"

"No!"

King could hear Buck Parnell's voice. *"You'll need gloves."* He didn't have any, and he wasn't sure how to let go of a wildcat. He gathered both her wrists into one hand and put his free arm around her waist to contain her struggles. She arched herself away from him, twisting in angry frustration. She was stronger than he would have expected, but he had the advantage in size and leverage.

"What have you got against Mrs. Parnell?" he asked conversationally.

"You big ox, let me GO! Mrs. Parnell! She's a — a harlot, that's what. She was one in St. Louis before Eli married her, and she's one still."

"Don't talk like a field hand. What's she done to you?"

"A field hand would have said she's a whore. I didn't call her that, even if that's what she is.

149

She's married to Eli and has her hooks out for every other man in town. Especially —" She stopped. "Even you," she finished. "First your brother, now you."

King heard that but set it aside for the moment. "That's not what you started to say. What difference does it make to you who Sheila —"

"Sheila?" she demanded. "Don't you mean Mrs. Parnell? Or is it Sheila now that you have her rouge all over your face?"

"All right." King sighed. He figured it was true. "I'm going to let you go. If you decide to hit me again, make it on the other side."

He backed away to arm's length and released her wrists. She stepped in at once, swinging straight and hard with a punch that would have done her dead brother credit. King slipped under it, bringing his shoulder up sharply into her midsection and lifting her off the floor.

"You shouldn't pick on people bigger than you," he said. "I do this for a living, and I outweigh you by at least fifty pounds."

Diana gasped for air, got her breath back, and began to pound at his ribs. "Put me down!" she cried.

"I ought to." He began to turn in slow circles. "First tell me the man you're so jealous of."

"Jealous? Stop that! I'm not jealous of any man on this earth."

"Not even Buck Parnell?"

"That's none of your affair."

King took her by the waist and set her on her

feet again. "Buck Parnell," he repeated.

"If you ever manhandle me again, I'll kill you."

"You have egg yolk on your chin."

"I don't!" She scrubbed savagely at her face. "You have egg on your nose. It's the only place you don't have rouge."

He pulled his sleeve across his face. "That better?"

"Worse." She scowled at him, bit her lip as a smile tugged hard at her mouth. "Here, I'll do it. Sit down."

"Never —" King began, but she was already searching for a rag. She pumped enough water to wet it and came back.

"Here. Sit down, I said. You have some splinters here, too, that have to come out. Where can I find a needle?"

King sighed and sat. Sheila Parnell's touch had been soft and gentle and seductive; Diana was briskly efficient, as though she were doctoring an injured horse. Before she was finished, he wished he'd taken the beating instead.

"Hold still. A harlot's rouge is hard to wash off."

"Worth remembering," King said. "How about an honest woman's rouge?"

Diana eyed him. The wildcat gleam was gone from her eyes. King hoped she wouldn't smile, but she did.

"I don't wear it," she said.

"I can see that."

He stood up. She didn't step back. Without

gloves, he put his hands on her shoulders and drew her nearer. She let herself be drawn. He bent to kiss her. It was the nicest sensation he could remember, but she only allowed herself to be kissed, taking it like a dose of medicine.

It came to King that twice that same night he'd been kissed by women who'd wished he was Buck Parnell. He didn't much like the idea. He released Diana, went to the cabinet, and broke a fresh egg over the dog's scraps. Without speaking, he took the bowl outside. The north wind was blowing, driving low dark clouds across the sky to hide the stars.

"Come inside." Diana Castleberry stood in the lighted doorway, urgency in her voice. "Are you begging somebody to shoot you?"

"Not your affair," King muttered, but he came inside because he was cold. And because she was right.

Diana closed the door and leaned against it, studying his face. "Thank you," she said after a moment.

"For what?"

"For being such a — such a gentle man."

He laughed, short and harsh. "I haven't shown it much tonight," he told her. "Nor since I've been in Willow Springs."

"But you have." She came to him, looked up into his face. "I didn't know. I thought men had to be rough and coarse.

King reached out for her again and enfolded her in his arms. She pressed her face against his

152

chest. Eyes closed, King drew a deep, ragged breath. *If I'd shot Buck Parnell every time I thought of it tonight,* he told himself, *my gun would be empty.*

Chapter 16

December 5, 1894

Cy Timm tripped over the barrels of his broken shotgun, recovered himself, and sped on as fast as he could manage by starlight. He felt he'd done well in a tight spot, talking to the Ranger, but all the same it was safest to get away. He had to think about what King had said. All that business about the letter — if there was a letter — was too deep for him to take in all at once. He hadn't written any letters, not even the one he'd thought to send to Eli. But unless King was lying —

Lost in his thoughts, Timm didn't see the dark figure looming from an alley. Not until someone grabbed his arm did he stop with a shrill squeak of fright.

"What did you tell him?"

"What — Judge!" Timm tried to shake loose from Blankenship's grip, then let himself be drawn into the deeper shadows. "I didn't say anything. Not a thing."

"Keep your voice down! What did you tell him?"

"I told you. Nothing. As God is my witness —"

154

"Yes, I heard that God was your witness. I also heard the word *beans*."

"No. I mean, King said that. He knows. He knows all about the beans and the drawing and that I got —"

Timm stopped himself with a shuddering effort. The judge was leaning close, his eyes glinting in the faint light.

"He knows," Timm repeated lamely. "But not from me."

"Then from whom?" Blankenship demanded. His grip tightened on the smaller man's arm. "You've forgotten our agreement — and what's at stake."

"I haven't forgotten anything. Not even that this was *your* idea from the start." Timm struck out with sudden strength, knocking the judge's hand aside. "It wasn't you facing him, and him mad enough to spit nails. Here I've done my best to shield you all, me taking all the chances, and much thanks I get for it."

"Be still!"

"I won't. He asked me about the beans. I denied everything, even when he threatened me. I risked my life lying to him."

Blankenship shoved him away. "You've risked your life, all right," he said.

"Don't you try to buffalo me, too. I know what's happened, right from the start. I was against changing the survey markers —"

"You fool, shut up."

"— and I was against killing Hollis. But I drew

your black bean and I was — I was ready to do my part." Timm paused for a deep breath, astonished at himself and at the feeling of power that seemed to flow from his anger. "But somebody jumped the gun. All your careful planning, and some jackass couldn't wait! I've kept our bargain, but I'm not so sure about you. After all, you're a great hand for writing letters."

Timm expected an explosion from the judge, even found himself looking forward to it. But Blankenship only stared at him, a slight frown creasing his high forehead.

"Letters? What do you mean?"

"That's how King knew about the drawing. Somebody sent a letter. He thought it was me, but it wasn't, as God's —"

"— your witness." Blankenship finished softly. His own anger had vanished and he was staring intently at Timm. "Did he say who else knew about the letter?"

"No. Or maybe he did, but I was too flustered to hear."

Timm sagged back against the wall of the building behind him. He felt weak and dizzy, but he didn't want Blankenship to see. "It had to be one of us, Judge," he said. "Who else could have known? But it wasn't me."

"Nor I," Blankenship murmured. "Who else indeed? And for what possible motive?"

Timm pulled himself erect. "You're the big planner and thinker," he said. "You just puzzle it out and let me know. I'm going home."

"Wait," Blankenship called, but Cy Timm was already out of the alley. He scurried a dozen steps toward his house, then slowed suddenly. With conscious care, he straightened his back and raised his eyes and stilled the trembling in his knees. With a calm, purposeful stride, he marched along the boardwalk and up the walk to his front door.

"Mattie," he called from the hallway. "Mrs. Timm, wake up! Come out here!"

"Mr. Timm?" Her voice was sleepy, puzzled. After a minute, she peered from the bedroom doorway, an old housecoat covering her nightdress. "Cyril, what on earth?"

Cy Timm put his arms around her and kissed her hard enough to hurt her lip. She stared at him in wonder, surprised but not displeased.

"Come to the kitchen, Mattie," he said. "Make us some coffee. I have a lot to tell you."

Chapter 17

December 6, 1894

At dawn, Jeff King took his carbine, left his brother's house, and strode along the weedy path toward the square. Abruptly he turned north and picked his way along an alley strewn with brush and trash. Emerging at the far end, King crossed a better street and entered the Willow Springs depot before Henry Drumm saw him coming.

Drumm sat tipped back in his swivel chair, boots propped on his desk. If he was surprised to see King, his face did not give him away. He shifted forward so that his feet were on the floor, rolled the match he was chewing to the corner of his mouth, and nodded amiably.

"Morning, Ranger." He made a leisurely inspection of King's battered face and showed white teeth in a grin. "If I didn't know better, I'd say you'd gotten too close to a catfight. For a man that tangled with a shotgun, though, you look pretty good."

"Thanks." King laid his Winchester across the counter. "Much as I value your opinion, that's not why I came."

Drumm raised his eyebrows. "Want to buy a

ticket someplace? I hope you're not leaving us already." His voice was so even that he might have been serious.

"Pretty soon. Right now I wish you'd send a telegram for me."

Drumm pitched the match toward the wastebasket and selected a fresh one from a box on his desk. He rose slowly and came to the counter, pausing to pour himself a fresh cup of coffee on the way.

"Care for a cup? I always make plenty." Smiling a little at King's headshake, he pushed a pencil and a yellow telegraph pad toward him. "Guess it hurts to drink with your face cut up like that. Too bad. A telegram, huh? Write it down for me."

King pushed the pad back to Drumm. "You look like an educated man. You set it down. Being that the town doesn't have a newspaper, I figure telling you is the quickest way to spread a story around."

"Could be," Drumm said. He grinned again and stroked his beard. "You're the customer. Go ahead."

"To: Captain John Slater."

Drumm bit his match until it angled up against his nose. "Fine," he said. He licked the pencil lead and began writing. "What address?"

"Care of the Adjutant General. Austin City."

"What message?"

"Tell him this. 'Good news. Know who. Know why. Rest soon.'"

"Was that 'rest'?"

King nodded. "If I'd said 'arrest,' it'd have been an *s* on the end of it. How much?"

"Four bits'll cover it."

King figured Drumm was staying at least even in the game they were playing. Maybe it was time to cut the deck. He took a half-dollar from his coat pocket and palmed it loudly on the counter. When he lifted his hand, a black bean lay on the polished wood beside the silver coin.

Drumm adjusted his match. Then he withdrew a white bean from his watch pocket, laid it beside the black one, and picked up the coin. "Call," he said.

King smiled. He couldn't help it. "I'll wait till the rest ante," he said. "But I can tell you now, you'd better take a new hand. When I turn my cards over, you're going to see four deuces and a joker."

The stationmaster widened his grin a bit. "My old man always said I should be sure I'd taken the pot before I counted my winnings. Seemed like good advice." Still grinning, he turned to his key and began tapping it.

King listened to the singing of the telegraph key until he was satisfied that Drumm had sent the right message. Then he went on toward the town square. He'd done all he could at the depot. He had a pretty good idea that, whatever he learned about the goings-on in Willow Springs, he wasn't going to learn much of it from Henry Drumm.

Pausing at the edge of the square, King watched as the sun began to light the faces of the buildings. He took an interest in Cyril Timm waiting in the shadowed alley beside Eli Parnell's store. A minute later, Buck Parnell came stalking toward the dark courthouse. King wondered at all the early morning activity. It put him in mind of a pot of stew beginning to bubble on the stove. Time pressed on him as Slater's deadline ticked closer. He had to do something. Maybe he could stoke up the fire.

He looked along the street behind him and then walked in long easy strides across the lawn to meet the new sheriff at the east door.

"Morning," he said.

Buck Parnell reacted to King's voice the way he might have responded to the buzz of a rattlesnake. "What the hell are you doing here?" he demanded.

"Now that we've got the niceties out of the way," King said, "I can tell you. I'm here to have a look at the sheriff's office."

"Why?"

"Because this is where it is."

"Look, friend, I don't feel like a lot of foolishness today. I'm asking you what do you want to see it for?"

King started to answer, then lost patience. "My reasons aren't any of your business. All you need do is unlock the door for me."

"Like hell I will." Parnell bowed his neck and

lowered his hand toward his holster.

King said, "Twice now you've roostered up at me in public, and twice I've let it go by. Right now we don't have any audience. If you twitch your hand any closer to that shiny gun, I might just have to kill you."

Buck stared at him, long and level. King saw caution in his eyes but nothing that looked like fear. He could kill Buck if he wanted it that way, he realized — or get himself killed instead. It would be easy enough to corner Buck in public where his touchy rooster's pride wouldn't let him back down. If King wanted it that way.

"That gun on your hip is a tool, Jeff Davis," C.D.'s voice echoed from some long-ago talk. *"Trouble is, you don't get no second chances with it. Before you take to use it on a man, be good and damn sure you want him dead."*

King didn't wait for Buck to make up his mind. "All right," he said. "You look real close at this badge. I'm a state official with legal right to look in the office where a murder happened."

For a moment longer, Buck Parnell stood red-faced, his eyes dark with anger. Then he seemed to come of age, to understand his position. He smiled, relaxed, hooked his thumbs behind his belt buckle. "Hell, friend," he said, "why didn't you put it like that in the first place? But I'd best ask the judge about you looking around the office."

"Judge keeps the key, does he?"

Buck colored again. "Why hell no! I'm sheriff

of this county. I carry my own keys."

"Use them, then. If I steal any county property, you can arrest me."

Parnell unlocked the courthouse door and went in. The two of them climbed the stairs to the first floor and entered the sheriff's office. Someone had cleaned the room but not very well. The wall behind the desk was stained. In one corner bright splinters sparkled in the sunlight. "Is that glass?" King asked.

Buck looked. "From the window," he said. "One charge busted it from hell to breakfast. The first one, I guess. The other took Hollis right in the brisket." He hesitated, and when he spoke again, his tone had changed. "I saw what it did to him," he said. "Hell of a thing."

King laughed, anger riding him hard and hot. "Sounds like you were one of the mourners," he snapped.

Buck looked at him soberly. "Listen, friend, I didn't have any use for Hollis, and I don't have much for you. But I wouldn't wish that on anybody."

"You might have wished it on yourself."

"That a threat, friend?" Buck grinned suddenly. "No call for two officers of the law to be threatening one another. But if I do need to fight you, it won't be with any shotgun. That's no weapon for a man to use." He shook his head impatiently, as if realizing he'd let down his guard. "That damned Crow's supposed to've cleaned the place. Can't trust him unless you're

163

watching him! I'll make him sweep that up if it —"

"Obliged," King cut in, managing to keep his voice level. "This'll take me awhile. Why don't you go get yourself some breakfast?"

"Had breakfast. Why don't I just stay here and watch what you do." He barked a laugh, and dropped into the chair behind the desk. "I'm still learning sheriffing. Might be good for me to see how a real nickel-plated Texas Ranger works."

"Might be. Is that where C.D. was sitting when he was shot?"

"I wouldn't know," Buck said. He leaned back in the chair, pointedly making himself comfortable. "I expect so, though he was on the floor when they found him."

"Who is 'they'?"

"Hell. The judge was the first one here. He saw how it was. Ask him."

King nodded. "I'll do that. But right now I'll have his gun," King said.

"What?"

"My brother's forty-five. It was his personal property. Been in the family awhile. I'd like to have it."

"I expect you would," Buck agreed. "I'll tell you the truth, friend, I haven't seen it since the night of the killing. Judge likely gave it to Hollis's wife before she pulled out."

"I don't figure he did."

Buck shrugged. "Well, *I* don't have it, and don't want it. Doesn't seem like it brought Hollis

164

much luck. Old piece it was, about half worn out."

"But it was here?"

"Sure. I picked it up, checked the loads, put it right there. Ain't seen it since." He shrugged again. "Hell! Ask Felder. That's the undertaker. Likely wouldn't be the first corpse he's robbed."

"Mind if I open a few drawers?"

"Why?"

"He might have a left a few personal things."

"Sure did. The judge, he gathered up everything that wasn't bloody and gave it to the widow. You can look if you like. You'll see what I mean," Buck squinted at him, then opened a drawer in the desk, "I do have one thing that was his." He extended his hand, the mangled badge lying on his palm. "Didn't figure his missus would want it. It didn't bring him much luck, either."

King took it, looked, put it carefully in his coat pocket. He turned away from Buck, his fists balled in sick, helpless fury. This time it was easier to control, and after a moment, he wheeled back to the desk. Somebody had already gone through the drawers as carefully as a tax collector. Not the one who had swept the floor.

"I'm looking for his fountain pen mostly. Always carried a silver one."

"Ask Felder."

"I don't guess you found his notebook either?"

"Notebook?" Parnell looked up quickly. "What kind of notebook?"

"He always kept one — don't you? Kind of a record of what was going on in his jurisdiction. Names and dates, things like that. For evidence in case anything happened to him."

"Hell!" Buck said. He bit his lip, then looked suspiciously at King. "What makes you so sure there was a notebook? What'd it look like?"

"I'll ask Felder. It could be that he reads." King turned toward the door. "Maybe you ought to have somebody copy down your thoughts, just in case something sudden happens to you. And I wouldn't bother having that glass swept up."

"What? Why?"

"Probably be a fresh batch of broken glass in here pretty soon. Cuervo can sweep it up all at once."

King left without looking back. In his mind he thought he could smell fresh wood sizzling under the stewpot. In his ears he could hear the harsh muttering of an angry man digging through piles of paper.

He came down the west stairs of the court-house and stood inside the door to look across at Eli Parnell's store. Timm was no longer out-side. King crossed onto the boardwalk so as to pass close in front of the store windows. Inside, he saw the little man holding a short-barreled Colt and talking to Eli Parnell. It would be a thing to remember that Timm carried a big-bore pistol. King thought about it all the way along to the newest building in Willow Springs.

The funeral parlor had been built of the same stone as the courthouse, probably by the same masons. It appeared to be the only really successful business in Willow Springs. King entered the wide door quietly, his hat in his hand. The hallway was carpeted in a solemn dark purple, the walls and ceiling painted white. King had admired the new building from outside, but now he noticed a fresh sandy brown stain that radiated out from the top of the wall to cover half the ceiling. However good a job the masons had done with the stone, the roofers had not been able to keep out the rain.

"Yes?" a man's voice called softly from one of the doorways. King turned that way and went into the office.

Hamilton Felder stood a hand taller than any horse or man in Blackrock County. King too looked up at him as the undertaker unfolded from his chair to loom behind a stout business desk. Though he was not much past forty, his hair was white as sugar. He reminded King of a man he'd seen in San Antonio, who'd been badly frightened by lightning. Felder had been whittling, carving tiny men and women from a hardwood stick. He put down his knife to offer King his hand and motion him to a chair.

"That's mighty fine work," King said.

"Thank you." Felder's voice was deep and husky, oddly hesitant. "I try to put back as much as I take."

167

"That's a good thought," King said. "They tell me you buried C.D. Hollis not long back."

"I prepared Sheriff Hollis's body. I surely did. Your brother, I believe. My condolences on your loss. But I surely did."

"I'm told he was shot in the back."

"That story went around, it surely did. But there was no truth in it. Not Sheriff Hollis. He was struck in the chest, a little to the left side."

"Would he have seen the one who shot him?"

"I think he must have, yes. By most accounts, he even fired a shot in return. Though how he could have done that, I don't know. A terrible wound, it surely was. People think it's buckshot does the work. But something smaller — say number four — does much more damage close up, it surely does."

"Why do you say by most accounts?"

"Some people said so. At the inquest. Heard three shots, they said. They heard the shotgun go off, once and then again before they heard the pistol. Didn't make much sense, surely didn't, until a fellow saw that the first shotgun charge missed the sheriff entirely and struck the wall up high."

"Two charges from the shotgun," King said, half to himself. It hadn't occurred to him that more than one man might have been involved. He just hadn't been thinking; five men had entered into the conspiracy. For all he knew, all five of them might have been there. "Who testified? Who said there were three shots?"

"Judge Blankenship, of course. And Bart Miller — they say you broke his nose. They surely do. Even Higginbotham, who was in his store that late at night. Cuervo heard the shots, I know. There isn't much he doesn't hear. But he didn't testify. He surely didn't. They didn't ask him."

"What about Hollis's gun? You should have known easy if it had a shot fired out of it."

"That was an interesting point. It surely was. The sheriff's pistol was missing. Majority opinion was that the killer took it."

"Who was in the office when you picked up the body?"

"Who? Judge Blankenship. My son Hardy. But of course he came with me. Who else was already there? Our present sheriff Buck Parnell. His brother Eli. Now that's a funny thing. I want to say that Henry Drumm was there. Of all people. But he wasn't. No, he —"

"What made you think of him then?"

"Of course." Felder looked pleased with himself. "I remember. He was at the other end of the hall, coming up the other stairs. But he never appeared in the office while I was there, he surely didn't."

"Then you arrived at the office and saw those other three."

"No. There were four. Blankenship, Parnell, Parnell, and Cuervo."

"Crow was there?"

"He surely was. He was straightening things

169

up in that office. The way he always did before Buck became sheriff."

"And you didn't see Hollis's pistol."

"No. The sheriff was wearing his holster but it was empty. I assumed someone had picked up his gun."

"And you saw no fountain pen? No notebook?"

"Oh yes. Those things were . . . were on his desk when I arrived, still there when I left. Silver pen, leather notebook. They surely were."

"Do you know what happened to them?"

Felder shook his head. King accepted it. He started to go, then changed his mind suddenly.

"I suppose you handled Donny Castleberry's body too."

Felder didn't like the new topic. He stared at the water stain on his new ceiling. "His body was here for a very short time. Sheriff Hollis brought it in himself. But Castleberrys don't bury here in town. Dallas came for Donny before dawn."

"You didn't prepare the body?"

"They have an old Mexican woman on the ranch does that for them. A *curandera*."

"Nothing you could tell about the body then?"

Hamilton Felder studied his desktop. "In confidence?"

King nodded. "Of course."

"The young man had been shot twice in the middle of his chest. You could have covered both of them with your hand. You surely could. He

170

must have died instantly."

"Yes?"

"The strange thing is, all the witnesses at the inquest testified Donny fired first. They surely did. The sheriff hadn't even drawn his pistol when Donny fired his first shot. And Donny was deadly with a handgun, he surely was."

"His first shot," King repeated. "How many were there?"

"Well, we surely don't know." Felder looked troubled. He leaned forward and spread his hands solemnly on the desk. "Didn't see it myself, you understand. And I hate to spread gossip. I have to live here."

King shrugged. "That's not gossip, it's public record. It'll be on file at the courthouse, and I can read it for myself." He straightened as if to rise, then looked at Felder. "You said you heard the shots?"

"Well, I can't recall saying that. But I surely did hear them. Five, I made it, but two came so close together it was hard to tell. And one —"

He stopped. King waited. The undertaker licked his lips. He seemed to be liking their conversation less by the moment. "Listen," he said. Little beads of sweat had appeared in the thin white sideburns in front of his ears. "I have to live here," he repeated.

King laughed sharply. "Or die here," he said just as sharply. He gestured toward the new walls of the building. "Lot of people seem to die here."

Felder wiped at the perspiration running down his cheeks. "Listen."

"I'm listening."

"It's not safe."

King pulled his coat back far enough to let light glint on his badge. "Since I've been here, about everyone I've met has lied to me about something or another," he said. "I'm hoping you'll tell me the truth. What about one of the shots?"

"I beg your pardon," Felder said soberly. "I didn't know your profession and position."

"You'd be the only one in town."

"I often am. Not too many folks run in here to pass the time of day." Hamilton Felder leaned closer to King. "It is my belief at least one of the shots was fired by a third party. It sounded different. I was not the only one to notice." He stopped and licked his lips again. "I — I do not believe it was aimed at Donny," he said finally. "I surely —"

"At who then? At Hollis?"

Felder nodded. "As I have put it together from the remarks of others, I believe that it was, yes."

"These others, do they think the same as you?"

"Not at all. Mostly they agreed to four shots. Two light, two heavy."

"Mostly?"

"Some said five. But there were only two shots missing out of each pistol."

"What did you say?"

"Me? I didn't testify. No one asked me to."

"But you heard five."

"I did. But I was inside. Right here. Yes I surely was." He shifted uneasily in the heavy chair. "I'm no expert on the sound of gunfire."

"And you have to live here. You surely do." King watched Felder wipe at the sweat on his face. "Did you tell Sheriff Hollis about the other shot?"

"Think about it now. *I* wasn't out there when the shooting took place. How did I know but that it was Hollis's first shot, before Donny opened fire? Or that he hadn't posted someone to back him up?"

"Now you're not talking about a gunfight. You're describing a murder."

Felder looked down at the desk without answering.

"You thought that little of Sheriff Hollis?" King asked. "You'd believe he set a trap to kill Donny?"

The tall man didn't meet King's eyes. "Some think that's why he was brought here," he said. "I don't know."

"Then you oughtn't to say it."

Felder looked at his visitor, measuring the change in his voice. "You asked for the truth," he reminded King. "I'll ask you a question: how long had it been since you'd seen your brother?"

It has long been in my Mind to Write. Best we put aside our differences while there is Time.

"Several years."

"Are you so sure he was the way you remem-

173

bered him? Men do change."

"*Stock detective.*"

The words came back to King from his child-hood, overheard by accident, not meant for his ears, half understood.

"*Stock detective, hell. Another name for bush-whacker, if you ask me.*"

"*Hush, now. There's his brother.*"

"Not Hollis," King said to both Felder and the memory. "I'm sure as I need to be." He rose and offered his hand. "I appreciate your help, sir."

Outside the dim oppression of Felder's new building, King turned toward the square and the restaurant fronting on the courthouse. His entry brought a sudden hush to the place. Buck was at a table in the corner with a cup of coffee and an El Paso newspaper. He gave King a slow nod.

"Ranger."

"Sheriff."

Buck went back to his paper. King chose a table away from the windows and ordered steak and eggs from the nervous proprietor. While he ate, he thought about Felder's question. Even when he'd been young, before Hollis married, King hadn't known him well. He'd depended on him, idolized him, loved him. But he hadn't known him as a man. Could Hollis have bush-whacked Donny Castleberry? Captain Slater might have answered that question. King couldn't. And the answer didn't really matter to him.

"*We'll have to look after each other now, Jeff*

174

Davis. That's what brothers do."

"Señor King?"

King looked up. A Mexican boy of about eleven was looking at him with shy brown eyes.

"Sí."

"The *señorita* Castleberry sends you this."

He held out a folded slip of paper. King took it and offered a coin, but the boy shook his head quickly and darted away. King unfolded the note, conscious that Buck was watching. The sheriff's assumed indifference was gone, laid aside with the newspaper.

I called at the Hollis house but did not find you. Father asks you to the ranch. Please come. D.

King paid for the meal and left the restaurant. He paused on the boardwalk, then crossed to the courthouse, up the stone steps and through the tall main doorway. The whole way, he was conscious of Buck Parnell's gaze, angry and resentful, centered on his back.

Chapter 18

December 6, 1894

"I want to buy some things."

"Sure thing, Cy. Always glad to have a paying customer," Eli Parnell smiled his wooden smile and moved along the counter to where Timm was waiting. Then he glanced quickly around the store and leaned close to the smaller man.

"What happened last night? What's that Ranger want with you?"

"I want to look at your pistols."

"They're right there in the case where they've always been. Did you hear me? What — ?"

"I heard you. He wants to hang me."

"What?"

"Or you. Or Buck or Henry or the judge. Maybe the judge most of all. Or maybe all of us. 'Bound together in mutual culpability,' the way Homer said."

Parnell glanced around nervously. "Hold your tongue with those names. What's wrong with you? You're not yourself today."

"That's right. Let me see that one — the one with the short barrel."

"The sheriff's model? That's what they call it.

176

But I want to hear about last night."

"Sheriff's model?" Timm hefted the heavy revolver, pointed it toward a nail keg and squinted down the sights.

He laughed. "A sheriff's model Colt to go with the sheriff's horse. What caliber is it?"

"It's a forty-five. But it's not like the others. It doesn't —"

"It'll shoot, won't it?"

"Of course it'll shoot. But it doesn't have —"

"Never mind. I'll take it. And a box of cartridges." He laughed again. "You might want to get in some practice yourself."

"Cy! Are you drunk? I've never seen you like this. You aren't yourself."

"Oh, yes, I am myself. What does that come to, cash money?"

"Listen, about the Ranger —"

"You ask Homer about the Ranger. And be sure and ask him who killed Hollis — unless you already know."

"That's enough," Eli cried. "You're drunk or crazy for sure, and I'll not sell a gun to a crazy man."

Timm thrust the heavy pistol into his waistband, then reached to the ammunition shelf and took down a box of forty-fives. "Bet you will," he said. He enjoyed Eli's stricken stare as he deliberately loaded the gun. It pleased him to feel as tall as Eli Parnell.

He seated the sixth cartridge in the cylinder, snapped the loading gate closed, and let the Colt

177

fall into his coat pocket. Drawing a couple of bills from his wallet, he waved them at Parnell.

"I didn't know you were in the habit of carrying so much cash," Eli said, reaching automatically to take the money.

"I'm not in any habit," Timm said. He gave a high, squeaky chuckle and started toward the door. "I'm a new man. My own man."

"Wait. You want your change?"

Cy Timm stopped. "Of course." He turned back, smiling. "Of course I do. Only a crazy man wouldn't want his change."

Outside, Cy Timm pulled his hat brim down against the morning sun and strode across to the courthouse. He unlocked the County Clerk's office, went to his desk, and took up a sheaf of papers. He wanted his day's work done early. He meant to go home for lunch with Mattie, then ride out to practice with the stubby Colt that made him equal to any man.

Something white caught his eye. An envelope lay on the floor just inside the doorway. Had it been there when he came in? Most likely, he decided. In his excitement, he had probably just overlooked it. Someone had slipped it under the door after hours — a belated taxpayer, probably. Just another thing to attend to before he could leave.

He took up the envelope and turned it over, squinting at the thin penstrokes of the address. He should know that hand, he thought. Opening it, he unfolded the single page inside. For a moment as he read it, his hands twitched with remembered fear. Then he touched the Colt and the fear departed.

Of course. I should have known.

He read it again, slowly.

Cy
We'd best meet to talk about those beans. Come to the old way station on Leon Creek at sundown.

Timm laughed and locked the note in his safe. "I'll be there," he said aloud. "I'll be waiting for you, you son of a bitch."

Chapter 19

December 6, 1894

Jeff King ignored the outriders as he let his horse pick the way along Castleberry's road to the DC headquarters. King spent the time counting up his evidence and his suspicions. The first part didn't take long. But his suspicions were beginning to harden into certainty. He knew that the judge and the sheriff and the county clerk were conspirators. He was just as certain that a local merchant and the railroad stationmaster were in on it, though it was harder to understand what part they played. And he still had no idea what had set the five of them against C.D.

"Give me a rope and I know who to hang, Jeff Davis. It's ciphering out the evidence with a pencil and paper that's the hard part."

From there C.D. would have gone on to talk about lawyers and judges and trials, but that wasn't what the thought had reminded King of. He had the nagging sense that his mind had tried a door and had found it locked. Now the door was gone. The idea, whatever it was, had gotten away from him.

Why hell, he told himself, *I don't have sense enough to do this job!* Hadn't Slater tried to tell him? *A lawman ought not to try to find his brother's killers! C.D. deserved better.*

He shivered, feeling the wind freshen at his back. Looking round, he saw a wall of low, heavy clouds far off on the horizon, rolling south like tumbleweeds before the wind. He spoke to his horse, who understood and agreed immediately, and they went on toward headquarters at a brisk pace.

At the edge of the central basin, one of King's guards turned back, but the other began to move in. He had closed to within twenty yards by the time they came to the hitchrail near the barns. King recognized Octavio, the younger of Castleberry's shadows. It suited the vaquero to sit high on his horse and stare down as King tied off his roan at the rail. King ignored him.

"King!" Dallas Castleberrry came out onto the covered front porch of the ranch house. "Afraid I was going to miss you. Thanks for coming out. Emma's been asking for you — some woman's whim, but since she's so poorly, I'd hoped you wouldn't mind talking to her."

"My pleasure," King said, though he'd hoped for something more, something that might point him toward a new trail.

Castleberry strode down to meet him, sticking out a weathered hand. "Good. I appreciate it." Gray eyes studied King. "Are you getting anywhere with those heathens in town?"

"I think so. But I haven't got anything to take to a jury."

Castleberry snorted. "Time was we didn't worry much about juries out here."

"Times change."

"Men don't." The rancher hesitated. "Still. I'd almost wish you could leave this business be. Diana tells me somebody tried to kill you."

King shrugged. "Maybe. If that's what they intended, it didn't work."

"Um." Castleberry glanced at the mounted vaquero. "Octavio, lead out my horse if you will." To King he said, "I'm riding over by Huerfano Mesa. The hands think we're losing some stock over there. If you'll wait around, I'll see you at supper."

"Depends," King said. "I thank you for the offer, but my time's getting short."

The young Mexican brought out Castleberry's saddled mount and handed over the reins. Then he withdrew to his ground-reined horse and swung into the saddle again.

"There's more than one way to take that." Castleberry patted the neck of the tall gray horse. "The closer you get to where you're heading, the more chance somebody will try to stop you."

King grinned. "I hope so," he said. "That'll make the job a lot easier."

"There's another thing. Hollis and me, we were pretty much the same kind of old lobo wolf. I understood about him — up to a point. Chances are if you keep pushing, you'll learn

182

some things you don't like."

I already have. King thought. *But brothers look* after one another. Aloud, he said, "I appreciate what you're saying. But I mean to get C.D.'s killer. He'd have done the same for me."

The rancher nodded. "God's truth, he would. And he wouldn't have worried no jury about the problem, either." He swung aboard the gray and reached a hand down to King again. "Make yourself to home here. Poor hospitality to leave you like this, but I expect you'll be looked after."

He touched heels to the gray's flanks and rode out. King watched him go, frowning. Before, Castleberry had been eager to see him probe into the killing, eager to bring down his enemies in Willow Springs. Something had changed his mind. King wondered what it had been. He looked again at the idea that Castleberry was the killer, then shook his head. Castleberry had denied it, straight out and on his word. King didn't think the rancher was lying.

"Jeff?"

King turned. A young woman in a blue velvet dress had come out onto the porch. For a startled moment, he wondered if Diana had a sister he hadn't met. Then she came down the steps toward him and he knew better.

"What are you staring at?" Diana demanded.

"At a beautiful woman," King said. He looked away toward the barns and the dark vaquero. "For a second there, I thought you were someone else."

Her laughter teased him. "That's flattering! Do you always have such a way with words?"

"Usually. But that wasn't what I meant. You're always pretty. I mean I didn't recognize you until you spoke."

"No? That's worse yet!"

He was grateful he hadn't said *until you bit at me.* "I'm glad to see you."

"That's much nicer!" She took his arm and turned him toward the smaller barn. They passed within a dozen feet of the vaquero.

They had not taken many more steps before he whirled his horse past them, leaped down, and turned to confront them. Standing in their path like the statue of a youth too proud to expect long life, Octavio reminded King of a tall thin letter *A*. The boy was lean as a lightning rod, too young to realize the harm his stance invited. He wore an ivory-handled pistol on his right hip and its apparent mate in his green waist sash, turned for a left-handed draw.

"I think you are without honor," Octavio said.

Jeff King bristled, then mentally backed off a pace. He hadn't expected trouble at Castleberry's ranch, but he had to be ready for any snakes he plowed up. It was just possible that Octavio had killed Hollis out of a sense of loyalty to his employer. If so, the boy likely wouldn't hang fire at killing Hollis's brother for the same reason.

"You insult me, *hombre*," King told him quietly in Spanish. "Why do you ask to fight?"

The vaquero looked momentarily startled at

the words in his own language. Then his eyes narrowed with fresh anger. "You come to spy on us," he snapped. "You mean harm to the *Señor* Castleberry — perhaps to the *señorita* as well."

"No," King said. "Only to the man who killed my brother."

"Liar."

"Octavio," Diana put in firmly. "A little moment. I need your help."

The vaquero spoke to her but kept his acorn dark eyes on King. "He is without honor," he said again. "A Ranger. You will not walk alone with such a man."

"Tavio! I will do as I please." Diana Castleberry wasn't having any of his insubordination. King saw between them the conflict of immeasurably strong wills, the flint and the steel. "Bring me my gloves," the flint demanded.

The steel gestured sharply with his left hand. "I am no servant."

"No, *Hermosito*," she replied, her tone softening. "But as a special favor to me, *por favor?*"

King was learning. He recognized in Diana's voice the same unpracticed sweetness she'd shown him a moment earlier. Just as important, he had learned which hand Octavio would use when he went for a gun.

"I left them at the little iron gate up on the hill. Please bring them."

"You need no gloves for him," Octavio spat.

If King had been uncertain before, he had no doubt from that moment that the vaquero was in love with Diana. *Poor bastard,* King thought, not sure which of them he meant.

"*Por favor,*" Diana repeated softly.

Octavio understood his position. With a last level glare at King, he accepted it. Breaking from his statuesque stance, he strode to his horse, sprang into his saddle without using a stirrup, and spurred the tall mount sharply up the caliche road past the Castleberry house.

Diana took King's arm again. When she looked up into his face, he saw that she was pleased. "Come on," she said. "I've something to show you."

"You enjoyed that," he said.

Her smile was immediate and warm. "Shouldn't I have? Perhaps not. I'm sorry."

"Tell Octavio."

"Oh, I will." She put her other hand to his face. "Does it still hurt?"

"No." He'd forgotten about his injuries. Under her touch they burned like fresh fire. "Your medicine fixed me right up."

A voice hailed them from the smaller barn. "Miss Diana!" Constanzo Alvarez, the old saddlemaker, poked his round brown head through a window, grinning, beckoning. "Ah, and *Señor* King. Come in, *por favor*. I too have something to show to you."

At the door they met strong wholesome odors of new leather and freshly sawn wood. The saddler pointed to his workbench. On the bench stood two small new wooden saddle frames laced with shiny nails and smelling of fresh glue. "Ah, here, see! What will you think?"

Jeff King realized the saddles were intended for the sorrel colts, for his nephews, for his brother's boys. He remembered the trade with Castleberry and his earlier conversation with the saddler, but the recollection was vague, as if it had all happened years ago. "Good," he said. It was all he could think of. He put a hand out and stroked one of the hardwood cantles. "They will be very fine."

"And these will be the covers," Alvarez said proudly. He pointed to a little stack of skins. "I will put some of these ones here and some of those ones there so they will look both of them twins like the colts."

King was pleased. "You do good work."

Alvarez inclined his head slightly, accepting the praise as his due. *"Gracias, Senor."*

Diana smiled at Alvarez, then tugged at King's arm like an impatient child. "Come on," she told him. He said a quick farewell and allowed her to draw him toward the open back door. Before they reached it, Octavio came ripping into the barn. A pair of small black leather gloves hung from his waist sash. King was surprised; he hadn't supposed that there would have been any gloves to find. Diana seemed just as surprised. Then the vaquero in his proud haste made a mistake. With his left hand he grabbed at the gloves.

Before he tugged them free of the band, he saw Diana slung off to one side and found himself staring down the bore of King's pistol. It took his breath.

"Right there," King said. "Just hold steady. Move your off hand away from that pistol. *Now,* by God."

"No, Tavio!" Diana screamed. She had caught hold of the door to keep herself from falling. "No!"

But Octavio had frozen. He paid no attention to her words. Alvarez called out at the same time, but none of it seemed to touch the vaquero.

It didn't touch King either. He was ready to shoot, waiting for an excuse, all but wanting to shoot. The boy was putting himself up for it. "I'll ask you one time. Did you kill Sheriff Hollis?"

The question seemed to bite through Octavio's pride. For a little moment something reined back his fury, and he looked levelly into King's eyes. He shook his head. "No."

"Then take your hand away from the pistol."

"Listen," Diana said. She moved back toward King.

"Keep your distance," he said without looking at her.

A new voice broke upon the tension in the barn. In Spanish the voice laid itself on the young vaquero's shoulder like a warm firm hand.

King knew then what he had only supposed before, that Saul was Octavio's father. The older vaquero stepped into the barn behind King.

"It would please me very much for you to put away the *pistola,*" Saul said in King's ear.

"It would please me very much for him to take his hand away from his *pistola*," King said.

"*Por favor*," Saul said more softly. Octavio remained the proud young statue.

"I'm holding this hammer up with my thumb," King warned. "If you shoot me, I'll drop it. If you're fast enough to kill me, I'll still let it fall."

Saul Velasquez stepped forward so that King could see his empty hands. "No," he said.

"Don't get between us."

"This is my son. I *must* get between you."

King understood him. There wasn't much left to say.

Saul took another step nearer. Then, in a flash of movement, he turned and swiped his son's hand away from the ivory-handled pistol. King blinked. It came to him that he might have dropped the hammer if he'd been quick enough.

Octavio bridled, still proud and angry, but now Saul was between them, his back to King, speaking softly and rapidly to the younger man. After a dozen tense seconds, Octavio's shoulders slumped. He let his father turn him around and shepherd him out through the wide doorway.

King drew a deep breath, suddenly remembering he hadn't done so for some time. He had not yet put away his pistol when the two horsemen rode swiftly away.

Diana Castleberry stood regarding King as if he were a wild and dangerous animal that had crept into her barn. She watched as he holstered his gun, but she did not come any closer to him. "Come on," she said. She strode out the front of the barn and back toward the house.

He followed as far as the hitchrail. She was several feet ahead. "It's been a pleasure," he told her. He began untying his horse.

She said, "Wait. I'm sorry. I didn't want it to be like this."

He believed her. "No fault of yours. He took a disliking to me back on the square that first day we met. No use my riling him before I'm ready to make charges."

"You certainly won't need to bring any charges against Tavio or Saul. Not for Hollis. They had nothing to do with it."

"I'm sure you believe that."

"I *know* it." She stared at him, her dark eyes pools of doubt and trouble. Then she pressed her lips together and turned quickly away. "Please." The word came awkwardly, as if she hadn't practiced it much. "Please. Come walk with me. Noel can see to your horse."

King turned to watch the vaqueros still riding steadily away to disappear into the clouds covering the north. "All right."

She took the wagon track that wound up the hill behind the house. He fell in beside her. Apparently, Octavio had passed that way to get her gloves, because the road was scarred with raw deep gouges left by a hard-driven horse. King knew there was a sign for him in those big hoofprints, if only he could understand it.

"Quail," Diana was saying.

"What?"

"Quail," she said again. "Didn't you see them? A nice covey of Bob Whites. No, Goose! That way. To the south. Would you like to shoot?"

Yes, of course he would. But he had work to do. He would like to spend a day with Diana. But he had work to do.

"I'm not much of a hand with a shotgun."

She did not care about his work. She led him on up the road. To either side were stands of dead and drying sunflowers giving way to a thicker growth of sage. Large late-season doves flew high above them following the far ridge line. King thought it might be the closest he'd ever come to Paradise.

At its crest the ranch road ran out onto the flat rock slabs of the mesa top, then curved gently down into a wide shallow bowl surrounded by rocky ledges. Here the soil was deep enough that a dozen strong old live oaks clung to survival. In their shade stood a small adobe chapel, its bell tower rising above the twisted branches. A high fence of black-painted iron pickets surrounded it. King had time to see white crosses and gray granite markers inside the fence, and then the fresh north wind flung him and Diana along the white road toward the chapel.

King looked north. The cloud bank had reached the ranch headquarters, engulfed it, and roiled on up the hill, its leading edge already blanketing the lower pan of their road in a thick misty curtain.

"We're going to get wet," he called.

Laughing, Diana reached back to catch his hand. Her long skirts fluttered and snapped like a banner in the sudden drive of the wind. "Hurry," she cried and broke into a run. The first great heavy drops of rain had just begun to pelt them like slow slanting bullets when they reached the iron gate before the chapel.

"Inside!"

Diana fumbled with the latch and the gate swung back on oiled hinges. A moment later, the two of them were huddled in the low doorway, half sheltered from wind and rain by the tower.

King kept hold of Diana's hand, drew her round so that he could look into her black eyes before the coming storm should cover them in darkness. "Listen," he said.

Her lips formed a *"Yes?"* but he could not hear it above the moil of wind. He bent closer to her. She leaned up to him until their lips came together. He found no hesitation in her embrace this time, only a clinging warmth which made him feel that she cared for him. For him alone. He put his arms about her and drew her into him as far as she would fit.

The ocean of cloud caught up to them, covered their refuge, and rolled on to the south, leaving them lost in the dark sanctuary of its wake.

Chapter 20

December 6, 1894

When the black horse lost enthusiasm for the run, Timm brought him back to a canter and set his mind on the man he was going to meet. No wall of law stood between the two of them; no one would help or interfere. Timm knew they were not meeting to talk. The prospect that would have terrified him a week before now only sobered him.

The storm had swept land and sky clean, then passed on as suddenly as it had come. Low sunlight slanted beneath a bank of black cloud and a rainbow arched broad and bright above the eastern mesas. Perched confidently in the saddle, Timm let the black pick its own way among the muddy ruts of the road. The brisk cold wind stung his thin cheeks. He made to turn up the collar of his coat, then laughed and let it be. It was good to be alive and unafraid, riding to meet his destiny.

Crossing the overgrown ruts of the old coach road, he slowed the black to a walk and swung wide to circle the station. The stone building stood deserted, the wooden shake roof sagging, empty window frames staring blankly at the ocotillo and creosote bush that struggled up the walls. No one was in sight. That was as it should be. Timm was early, intentionally so. He didn't mean to take his enemy for granted. By the time he had made certain no horse or man lurked within two hundred yards of the station, he figured he had a half hour of daylight left to practice.

He tied the big black in a thicket along the creek and walked back, watchful, picking the marks he would shoot. Ten yards from the black doorway of the building, he whirled, pulling the Colt from his pocket and firing with clumsy haste at his six targets.

The pistol roared, bucked in his hand as he cocked the hammer, roared again. The noise was louder than he'd expected, a great hollow boom that hurt his ears, but Cy Timm didn't flinch. He had become the man so long hidden inside his timid body, a man no longer afraid. He wasn't surprised that four of his bullets had found their marks. When it counted, he would do better. Exultantly, Timm raised his face to the sky. *Come on, you son of a bitch,* he thought. *And come shooting. I'm ready for you!*

Almost negligently, he pulled a handful of fresh cartridges from his pocket. He'd seen other men reload their Peacemakers in a few seconds' time, and he knew he could do the same. He flipped open the loading gate and reached for the ejector rod. His finger slid smoothly down the bare steel barrel.

"Wait," he said, his picture of his own competence suddenly shaken. "That's not right."

But it was. He turned the pistol over, stared at it. A sheriff's model Colt, Eli had said.

"But it's not like the others," Timm heard Eli's dry voice saying as if the storekeeper were reading an obituary. *"It doesn't have —"*

"An ejector rod!" Timm finished aloud. "It doesn't have an ejector rod!"

He turned the Colt up and shook it. Bulged by the explosion of the gunpowder, the cartridge cases were stuck tight. Next he scrabbled in the mud for a stick and thrust it into the cylinder. The stick broke.

In the near distance, a horseman parted the curtain and jogged steadily through the dusk. Timm needn't have worried about concealment. The rider came straight up the old road at a steady, even pace, afraid of nothing. Water splashed upward around his mount's hooves. A long gun angled out from his saddlebow like a knight's lance.

Timm took a breath. He would never make it back to his horse. Nothing left but to make his fight in the best way he could. But that was how he'd wanted it. He was a man. His own man.

He ripped his penknife from his pocket and fumbled it open with sweat-slick fingers. He broke the first blade, then managed to snag the second under the lip of a fired cartridge. He levered out the spent shell and immediately stuffed a fresh one into the empty chamber.

No time for more. The rider had drawn within pistol range. The setting sun was in Timm's eyes, turning horse and man into a black-shadowed cutout against the orange clouds, but that didn't matter. However uncertain the light, the rider was too near for Timm to miss. Timm lifted the Colt and rocked the hammer back. With no thought of missing, he fired.

The hammer dropped on a spent cartridge with the sound of a brass bell. Timm cursed himself. Of course. He hadn't thought to spin the cylinder to bring up his one live round. No time now. He'd have to work around to it. Inexorable as a clock striking, the long gun slanted his way as the Colt snapped a second and third time.

"You little bastard," the rider said, soft and almost admiring. "I didn't think you had the sand."

The voice threw Cy Timm off. He knew it, of course, but it wasn't the one he was expecting. There was no hatred in it, no anger. He hesitated for the barest fraction of a second, his aim wavering as he looked into the horseman's eyes and suddenly saw the cold answer to all his questions. Then he set his jaw and tightened his grip on the Colt's handle.

Still standing game and solid, Cy Timm got off his only round just as the shotgun flamed at its muzzles and slammed a double load of shot squarely into his chest.

Chapter 21

December 6, 1894

For a time after it passed, Jeff King and Diana Castleberry remained mingled in the silent union which the storm had brought them. Finally, he tilted his head so that he could look into her face which rested against his lapel. Her dark eyes were closed, but he did not think she was asleep.

"I'm grateful for the rain," he told her softly. She opened one eye and rested it on his. "Are you?"

"It allowed me to be alone with you."

"The storm was our chaperone."

The idea made him smile. "Not a very good one," he said.

"Perhaps not."

"Listen."

"Yes?"

"The thing is, I don't know how much longer this job will take me."

She bent her head so that he could no longer see her face. "Is the job so important, then?"

"The most important thing — almost the most important thing — in the world."

"Almost?"

The word sounded teasing, but there was a deep seriousness in her voice. King frowned looking down at her dark head. "Yesterday I was in a hurry," he said. "I still am — I have to be. But now I won't be happy to leave."

"No?"

"No. I mean — damn it, but I haven't ever needed to say this kind of thing before. I don't have much practice."

"No?"

"No."

"A woman would be flattered — if she believed that."

"I don't plan to look for others to tell."

Diana pushed away from his chest and regarded him fully. In a new voice, she asked, "Then you really mean it?"

"Haven't found how to say it yet. But I do, yes. I mean it."

"We need more time."

"After I'm done."

"There are things you don't know."

"I'll learn them."

"And you like the DC?"

"Well — of course I do."

She smiled and pressed herself against him again, her arms sliding around his waist to hold him tightly. "Then let's forget everything that's happened — all the killing." Her voice was muffled against his shirt. "Let's start fresh, Jeff."

"Soon. In a couple more days —"

"No, not so long. Can't we begin now? Right now? From the storm?"

King held her, a tight ache building in his throat. "Diana, he was my brother."

"What am I?"

"You don't understand."

"Don't I!"

She flung herself out of his arms. In the moment before she turned away, King saw that her face was wet with tears. It surprised him, because he hadn't imagined anything could ever make her cry. She took two steps into the muddy churchyard and turned on him, pointing with a trembling hand toward one of the stones.

"Don't I? That's *my* brother there! Where they buried him after he — after *your* brother —" She stopped and covered her face with her hands. "It's my first day not to wear mourning," she said brokenly. "I was so happy because you — because you were coming."

He came up behind her and put his hands on her shoulders. For an instant he felt her muscles tense under his touch, and then she relaxed, allowing herself to be drawn back against him. "Diana," he said. "I'm sorry."

"The hard thing is, I wasn't here when he needed me. I was away. At school in the East, Mama's idea. I didn't even get back for almost two weeks after — afterward."

Of course. Diana Castleberry was the only other person in the world who could understand just how King felt. He knew people who would

have said fate had brought the two of them together because they had the same aches — but
not quite the same. Diana didn't have to think
about justice — or was it vengeance? The man
who had killed *her* brother was dead, buried deep
in Willow Springs.

"It's a hard country," King murmured.

He hadn't calculated it, but it turned out to
be the right thing to say. Diana straightened, not
pulling away from him but standing on her own,
a proud wild thing submitting to his gentling
touch.

"Yes." She nodded soberly toward the other
markers within the iron fence. "A hard country."

"These your people?"

"Mostly. Those two over in the corner were
here when Papa filed on the land. We don't know
who they were, but they must have loved this
place too. These by the chapel are the vaqueros
and their families, all the way back to the beginning of the DC." She hesitated, then gestured to
her right. "Here's the family plot."

Accustomed to counting by sixes to see how
many his pistol would cover, King noted almost
as many stones. "A lot of graves," he said.

"That's Dallas — my oldest brother. He was
killed by Apaches when he was 17, fighting for
the ranch the year I was born. Deke came right
after Papa and Mama settled here, before there
was a town or anything. He lived three weeks.
David isn't here, but that's his marker — he and
some vaqueros went after a gang of rustlers when

I was nine. None of them ever came back." She stood silently for a moment. "You already know about Donny. The big stone is for Papa and Mama — someday."

King didn't say anything. After a moment, Diana turned and looked solemnly into his face. "All those sons," she said, "and I'm the only one left. Papa was counting on Donny to take over from him."

"And now he's counting on you?"

"Yes."

"Is the ranch so important, then?"

"Yes! The most important thing in the world!" She swept a hand toward the graves. "It's my life and my land — Castleberry land! And there's thirty families, more than a hundred people, who have their lives here and their dead buried on this hill. It's like a —"

"Kingdom," King finished softly. Before, he'd seen only her beauty and her spirit, things that might have come from her mother. Now he could see her father in her, determination and strength and fierce imperious pride. "Is your mother's health better?" he asked. "I understood she'd been ill for some time."

"She's been ill for years," Diana said. "I wish you could have met her before. When I was a little girl, I thought she was beautiful. She had raven black hair."

King leaned down and kissed her softly. "She must've been very beautiful," he said, "to birth a daughter like you."

"But Donny was her favorite — her last son," King tasted the bitterness in Diana's flat tone. "Since he — died — she's just given up." She raised her head defiantly. "I'll never do that — not till God Himself takes me. I'll not just fold up like an old spider and die!"

King held her tight. "I do —" he said "— do *admire* you for that."

"Do you?" She turned to him, mischief in her eyes. Whatever trouble hid there had gone away for the moment. "I don't believe I've ever been *admired* before."

They walked back through the little cemetery and down toward the house. The swift glancing rain had penetrated little deeper than the top layer of white powdery dust on the road. The young couple's tracks ran close along together, quick and dark and already fading by the time they stepped onto the front porch.

"Listen," Diana said as King opened the door. "We'll make some gingerbread. Come on out to the kitchen with me."

"*Señorita.*" It was Socorro, waiting for them just inside. "*Un momentito, por favor.*" She drew Diana through the bead curtain into the hallway. They exchanged a few quick, hushed words in Spanish.

"Now?" Diana demanded.

"Yes, Miss Diana. The mistress says. And alone. She says alone."

"Very well! Thank you, Socorro."

Diana swished back through the bead curtain

with black fire in her eyes. "Come on, then," she said to King.

He took the hand she held out to him and followed her to the foot of the stairs. "Go on up," she said. "Mama wants to see you."

"Aren't you coming with me?"

"She wants to see you alone."

He went up the stairs, tapped at the dark door, and went in at the hest of Emma Castleberry's weak voice.

"Oh, Mr. King, good evening." Her luminous eyes smiled, though her lips hardly moved. "I'm so glad that you could come to finish our talk! Please, sit down. No, no. Over here in the light so I can see you."

"Evening, ma'am. I hope I find you in better health today," he said. But in his mind he saw again the trestle bearing a white-painted coffin.

"Yes," she said. "I feel much stronger today, thank you."

It took King back. Emma Castleberry seemed even more frail than he'd remembered, the skin of her wrinkled hands almost transparent. She did not look better, but he thought she had more of that Castleberry spirit than her daughter credited.

"I'm pleased to hear it," he said.

"I'm pleased you came to visit Diana." She turned her head to look out the window. "There was a storm."

"Yes," he said. From her tone, he thought she must know exactly how he had spent the storm.

"Did you enjoy it?"

"I did."

"That's good. In a dry land, a man must learn to appreciate storms. Look forward to them." She turned to smile at him once more. "It's a part of caring for the land."

"Yes ma'am."

"And my daughter? Do you care for her?"

Again the frail old woman surprised him, but he understood. He'd seen the haste of death before, the rush to get things in order. Sometimes he lived in that haste himself. "I do," he told her. "Very deeply."

"That's good. In a dry land, a man must have a strong woman —"

"And appreciate her."

"Yes. And a woman. A woman needs a strong man. Diana. If she's to run the ranch. Not alone. You must —"

Emma Castleberry closed her eyes. Against the pillow her hair was gray on gray. To King, the whole room was gray except for the coffin that he saw now and then in front of the fireplace. He looked through the curtained windowpane into the dark low aftermath of the storm. A slight movement at the crest of the hill caught his eye. Gray on gray, the movement grew into a man on horseback coming slowly, steadily, wearily down the long road toward the house. A stooped man wearing a gray slicker and riding a gray horse. Dallas Castleberry.

The gray woman stirred as if aware of her

husband's approach. But she couldn't have known, King thought. There was no sound above the wind, and only the best eyes could have found the rider.

"Mr. King."

"Ma'am?" He returned his full attention to her. She seemed rested by the pause. Her words came more strongly now.

"You didn't know my son."

"No, I'm sorry to say."

"Don't look so grim. It's — all right. It's all right. But I wonder whether you would do me a favor."

"Anything within my power."

She went on as if she had known what he would say. "I want you to deliver a little gift for me."

"Of course."

"Without asking why?"

He nodded.

"Without telling anyone? Especially not Dallas — not yet. He doesn't know."

"I have many faults —"

"Yes," she cried, "I can see that! They're wonderful."

"Ma'am?"

"But unnatural curiosity isn't among them."

"No, ma'am."

"Open the drawer in that writing desk. The package wrapped in that lilac handkerchief. Put it away on your person where no one will see it."

The handkerchief was neatly wrapped around

the contents and then tied where all four corners came together. He put it in his coat pocket. "Where do I take it?"

"Where?" She stared at him. "That's right, you wouldn't know, would you?"

He shook his head. In the far yard below, the gray horseman entered the long barn. "No, I don't know who it's for."

She gestured to him until he came near. Then she lifted a hand to his shoulder and drew him down to her with amazing strength. "To *Maria*," she whispered warmly in his ear. "Maria Perez. Ask Cuervo." She turned her head slightly to move her gray lips from his ear so that she could kiss his cheek. "Thank you," she whispered. "I'm sure you — and Diana —"

Her left hand slipped from his shoulder. "— could —"

"What?"

"*Vaya con . . .*" But her eyes were closed, her face relaxed in exhaustion, her breathing light and shallow. King looked down at her a moment longer, then left the room softly so as not to wake her. In his pocket and in his mind, the square package was a nagging weight.

Diana waited for him at the foot of the stairs. She held a silver tray on which stood a tall coffeepot steaming at the spout. "Well?" she said softly.

Her warm question was King's first test and temptation. "She wanted to know whether I like

206

it here." He followed Diana into the den and sat where she pointed.

"And what did you answer her?"

"That I'd be especially partial to the country, except that the women are so hard to get to know."

"Ha!" She put down the tray, came to King in two long strides, and perched herself on his lap. "And what was her response to that lie?"

"She kissed me. Seems like it runs in the family."

Diana put her arms about his neck and kissed him as if they were the only two people on earth. While they were lost in the kiss, Dallas Castleberry came in the front door steaming from the rain and stamping mud off his boots; and a surprisingly tall gray woman swished through the hallway bead curtain to confront them all in her nightclothes. King stood up out of the leather chair, holding Diana until she could get her feet beneath her. Dallas Castleberry gave them a quick, searching glance, then turned to stare at his wife.

Emma Castleberry wore tall brown riding boots and a wide leather belt cinched over her nightdress. She apparently saw no one but Jeff King. To him she said, "There's danger there. That's how they killed my boy. Come on! I'll go with you. We'll ride —"

She had just begun to topple forward when Dallas Castleberry made it across the room to catch her in his arms. "God Almighty," he said, to King or to Diana or to them both. "Can't I leave you by yourselves for one hour without —" However he may have meant to describe the scene he'd entered, he let it die in his throat. Gently he lifted the frail woman and carried her out of the room and up the stairs. "Socorro! Socorro, come help!"

Jeff King and Diana Castleberry turned half away from each other. "I'd better talk to him," he said.

"No." She started to turn his way, then looked anxiously up the stairs. "It's better if you go now. I'll see you soon. We have to decide —"

"Decide what?"

"Decide what — we're going to do, you and I. Decide what to tell him."

"I know what I want to do. As soon as this is over —"

She turned away abruptly and he knew he'd said the wrong thing. "It's not what — it's not as easy as you think. I need to get up there now. Please go. Please, Jeff."

"I hate to leave it this way," he said.

She said, "Never mind"; but he saw that she didn't mean it, that he had somehow ruined everything. She was not looking at him, no longer thinking of him. He found his hat and left her. By the time he reached the rim of the hill, King was looking for the vaqueros, ready to shoot it out with them or fight them bare-knuckled. But all the way back to town he never saw a living soul.

Chapter 22

December 7, 1894

Cuervo paused halfway across the cemetery to kneel beside the largest tombstone. He had dug the grave and set the stone himself. Although he could not read the inscription, he knew what it said: *C.D. Hollis and Beloved Husband* with the dates and below, in different script, *Assassinated.* As he rested there with his head down, he looked like a man lost in contemplation or prayer at the foot of the stone. In fact he was quite actively studying all the ground within rifle range.

Though his ears were not so sharp as they'd once been, he had heard a sound behind him as he shambled along the rutted road from town, a distant clink of metal on metal. Not so long ago, he thought, his ears would have warned him of danger and his eyes would have spotted the source like a raven's spying out a fresh carcass. Now he had to kneel like a ragged priest and peer between his fingers in the hope of seeing movement.

But whatever had made the noise — man or mockingbird or donkey — was not now moving. Cuervo saw nothing in the cemetery, nothing beyond the low stone fence except rain-dark sage swaying in the sharp north wind. Straightening, he put on his hat, and hopped on across that hallowed ground toward the far fence.

There he unlocked an unpainted wooden shed hidden by a tall stand of ocotillo from the front gate. He latched the door, waited a moment for his eyes to learn the dark, and then peered through the crack at the edge of the door. Nothing moved within his field of view.

With a quick, impatient jerk of his head, Cuervo turned away. He lit a lamp in the daytime darkness of his shed and moved to the little workbench. His shovel lay waiting for him. Soon it would need a new handle. He thought of replacing it, but he did not like to waste the last of the old handle by putting in a new one too soon.

Instead he took up a file and began slowly and thoughtfully to sharpen the shovel's blade. It wasn't smart to work with dull tools. But neither was it wise to wear out a file from too much heat. He worked wisely. The events of the last few days needed their chance to turn round in his head until they fitted together.

There was King, the new man, the Ranger. Cuervo tried to think why he liked King. In the old days when his ears were better, he had been shot at often by Rangers. Of course, he had shot back in his turn. He had told the new man King about the Rangers and Apache buried on this very same sacred hill. But King hadn't understood.

Maybe it was when King told them he was the brother of the real sheriff Hollis that Cuervo decided he didn't dislike him. Hollis had been a strong man, if not as sly as some. Mostly, Cuervo had as little use for sheriff's as for Rangers, but he had liked Hollis.

Did it matter that these brothers' names weren't the same? Cuervo cocked his head and squinted at the question, his file momentarily still. Most likely King had picked his name for himself, making up one he thought fit better than the name he'd been born to. Cuervo could find no fault with the idea, because he'd done the same himself. Maybe King behaved the way he did because of his name, just the way Cuervo enjoyed being the crow. At the thought, he let go a little cawing laugh.

He held up the shovel and examined its blade in the lamplight. The handle was worn and a new one stood by the door, but Cuervo decided to wait. There was a bit of good left in the old one still. Outside the dirt was waiting to be turned. Cuervo had the feeling that someone would need a new grave very soon, but he had a stronger feeling about the noise he'd heard on his way to the cemetery. He knew that noise. He tried to remember, but the only memory that came was of the night they'd killed the young Castleberry.

That day, Donny had been sitting in the back room of the Lost Mule drinking tequila when he should have been on his way to the border. It was good that he stayed out of sight, because he had enemies — his father's enemies and his own — in town, and he'd shaken off the two vaqueros that the Old Castleberry always had ride with him; but it was bad that he was in town at all, and worse that he was drinking.

"Best thing is you'd be on your way," Crow remembered saying. "Plenty of time to drink when's you're there — if that's the best thing you can think to do, caw-haw-cawf."

For a moment, Donny Castleberry had looked at him with a cold and challenging stare. Donny was as blond as his sister was dark, a tall, lean, hard-muscled young man with a yellow beard as short as his temper and summer-sky eyes and a mouth that could widen into a boy's grin or narrow to a thin dangerous slit. He half-rose, but then remembered it was only Crow talking and relaxed back into his chair. "You know better than that, old bird." he said as he settled back into the chair. "You'd know better than most. I'm waiting for my lady."

"Caw!"

"Don't caw at me, old blackeyes. You know why we have to wait for darkness."

"God meant the day for traveling, caw-haw. You've ciphered out for yourself what He made the nights for. Best you all get riding, get as far from here as you can. Your papa —"

"I don't aim to go far tonight. We'll be moving slow."

"More's the pity, then. Your papa, he'll be fit to tie a goat. Those vaqueros supposed to be

212

watching out for you, he'll take a piece out of them you could use to bait a bear trap, caw-cawf. They'll come searching and spying you out before you and your missy gets anywhere near where you're going."

The long speech used up Crow's breath and he fell into a fit of coughing. Donny waited, grinning, until he fell silent and wiped his round watery eyes.

"I don't think they will," he said then. "Not for two reasons will they figure I'm headed for the border."

"No?"

"No. First reason is they won't think to follow wagon tracks."

"Not less'n somebody tells them what to look for, maybe. But your papa, he's got his eyes and ears all over this town."

"Not everywhere," Donny said. "I've kept one secret from him, anyway."

"Ain't —"

"Second reason," Donny interrupted, "is you're gonna tell them which way to look — the wrong way."

"Ain't smart to lie to your papa. Smart man wouldn't think about that, caw-haw."

"I had a fight with my pa before I left the DC. When somebody comes looking, you'll say I rode north to paint the saloons and the whorehouse at Tascosa. Pa'll believe that right enough."

"Caw-haw, not me. Not me, no. Your papa, he's treated me mighty good, mighty good, caw!

Why would I tell him wrong?"

"Maria. And me. We need your help."

Crow sat back and cocked his head and blinked his round black eyes. When he couldn't think how to answer right away, Donny went on, soft and serious.

"It ain't forever, old bird. We'll come back when the time's right. Likely Pa won't hold it against me when he knows the truth — my ma will see to that. But it's coming to bloodshed, what with the crowd in town and us and Hollis all packing iron and looking for trouble. The way things are, I can't have Maria in the middle of it."

"Hollis — caw-haw-haw-cawf —" Crow took a drink and wiped his eyes and started again. "The sheriff, he ain't against you. Him and your pa's as good as friends."

"Maybe. But he's not my friend. I don't trust him no more than the rest of them." He held up a hand when Crow started to protest. "I know you think I'm wrong. But I still need your help, for Maria."

"Cawwwwww." That was true, of course. But he wished Maria would go on with her little Castleberry right then so that they could get to the border. The town was full of dangers for Donny. There was Ramon Olivas who loved her too and would kill for her if he knew. And there were enemies of the Old Castleberry, any of whom would rather kill the boy than eat supper.

"Hey, you — Cuervo!" Horace Winkler, the

Lost Mule's proprietor, stuck his head through the doorway. "We got customers. There's tables to clean. Get yourself in here, less'n you're too drunk to use a broom."

But Crow hadn't been drunk then. He doubted any man could work around the bottles without uncorking one now and then. But he knew that he was not drunk because he understood what the word meant. Drunk, he knew no words, heard no sounds. Shaking his head and muttering, he went to tend to the saloon's business.

When he returned, things had changed. Donny was still sprawled back in his chair, a glass loosely cradled in his hand; but the alley door was ajar and Buck Parnell sat across the table from Donny. Buck was pouring their glasses full of the good tequila.

"You'd better grab up that girl and get the hell out of town, friend," he was saying. "I'm telling you for your own good."

"When did you get so interested in my good?"

Buck shrugged. "Believe what you want to. But if Hollis finds out, he won't let you take her without a fight. Not if what he's been saying is true."

"Did you hear him say that?"

"Lots of people did. He's not kept it no secret."

"That he's been lying with her? It's a dirty black lie!"

Buck shrugged again. "Don't roar up at me. I believe you," he said. "Don't make any difference what other folks think."

215

"Listen," Crow said.

"What the hell!" said Buck. "This is a private conversation. Get on about your business."

Crow stared at Buck with one black eye, then ignored him. To Castleberry he said, "You know she wouldn't. It's a lie."

"I'll kill him!"

"No," said Crow. "You don't want to kill anybody now. You want to take your girl and go."

Buck rose and came over to Crow, draping his long heavy arm across Crow's shoulders. "Listen," he said very quietly. "You got to help in this thing, see? So's Donny don't get killed. You need to mix up some of that Mexican horsefly stuff for Donny." He walked Crow back through the door into the bar. "Don't make out like you don't know what I'm talking about. You mix it up and get Donny to drink it. That'll quiet him down so's he'll go."

"Go?"

"Why hell, yes, go. What'd you think?"

Crow knew what Buck meant. A little special powder mixed with the tequila would make Donny sleepy. Crow was puzzled, because he hadn't trusted Buck, but it was a good idea. He didn't like to give the horsefly to a friend — sometimes it made a man wild instead of sleepy — but he made up a little bottle of it anyway. If Donny wouldn't take it, he would drink it himself to take away the need to think.

"You in there, Crow!" Buck called. "Hurry up!"

"I mean to kill him before I go," Donny's voice said faintly. "Where is the son of a bitch?"

"Whoa down a minute there, friend. Let's have another drink first. Crow!"

Crow knew something was wrong, but he couldn't think what to do. There was no time. Buck was calling him, throwing words, making sounds. He took a strong gulp from the horsefly bottle, then turned to carry the rest of it into the back room.

Crow's thoughts had carried the grave along. It was past knee-deep when his ears heard movement again and called him back from Donny. He climbed out of the narrow trench and leaned against a tombstone, his eyes busy while his fingers rolled a Christmas candy cigarette. As he put it to his mouth, he finally saw what he'd been seeking — the glint of metal where none should be. With the upward jerk of a crow taking flight, he straightened and turned toward the shed, but then the big heavy droning bullet struck him and knocked him into the grave.

Chapter 23

December 7, 1894

King gave himself time for a good breakfast and the town time to get its business running. He had spent much of a sleepless night alternating thoughts of Diana and the situation at the DC with thoughts of the conspirators in Willow Springs. He could see no immediate way to repair the situation with Diana and her family; that was a personal matter, one that would have to wait until his other business was finished. In spite of what Diana had said, he was sure they could work things out once he'd found Hollis's killer.

Finding the killer was a problem he knew how to handle. Proof was still lacking, but the stew pot was bubbling right along. If he kept adding heat, things would boil over sooner or later. Stacking his dishes in the dry sink and taking up his carbine, he went to stoke up the fire.

The westbound morning train was pulling into town, its locomotive belching great clouds of smoke and steam, as King strode by the station. Reaching the town square, he entered the courthouse and went straight to the County Clerk's office. The door was closed but unlocked. King grinned and pushed through the door, then stopped dead in surprise. He'd expected to find Cy Timm, but instead two middle-aged women waited inside, one of them at Timm's desk and the other sitting on a wooden bench beside the door. Both looked up eagerly as he entered.

"Have you —" the woman behind the desk began. Then she saw who he was and the light went out of her face. "I'm sorry. We were expecting someone else."

"Ma'am," King said. He removed his hat. "Are you waiting to see Mr. Timm?"

"We are awaiting news of Mr. Timm," the second woman said. She was tall and slender, neatly dressed in somber gray, and her white hair was pulled back in a severe bun at the nape of her neck. "This is Mrs. Timm," she said with a graceful gesture toward the woman behind the desk. "I am Mrs. Blankenship. May I ask your name?"

"Jeff King, ma'am. Is anything wrong?"

"I suppose you're that Ranger Mr. Timm has been telling me about," Timm's wife said. "I can see no harm in your knowing. Mr. Timm did not come home last night. The sheriff and Judge Blankenship are inquiring into the matter. We are waiting here in case he should return."

King stared at her. "Did —" he began, then stopped. "Pardon me, but is it unusual for him to stay out this way?"

"We have been married twenty-eight years," she said. "Just after he came back from the War.

219

In all that time since, he's never done anything like this." She smiled slightly. "He failed to come home for lunch in June of eighty-eight. He still won't say why, and I still haven't forgiven him. I am very concerned."

"I see." King said. He tried to picture Timm as he must have been twenty-eight years ago, just after the War. "Maybe he's been under a strain lately."

Mrs. Blankenship stood up from the bench. She was very nearly as tall as King. "Are you the strain, Mr. King?"

"No, Ma'am. I'm the ease."

"Pardon?"

"All he has to do is come and talk to me." He hesitated, then said, "I suppose the judge has told you what I'm doing here."

"No. Homer never brings the county's business home with him. Nor would I wish him to do so." She gave King a close, level scrutiny. "The town gossips say that you are here to find the killer of that awful Sheriff Hollis and that you suspect my husband. I am sure you're wrong."

"Yes, ma'am. Do you have an idea who the killer might be, then?"

"No. But my belief —" she glanced at Mrs. Timm. "— *our* belief is that whoever did it was God's instrument, avenging the wrongs he'd done."

Without his realizing it, King had tightened his grip on his hat brim until his knuckles were white. He waited until he could unclench his fingers and could hold his voice perfectly steady.

"Did the town gossips tell you Sheriff Hollis was my brother?"

He heard Mrs. Timm's quick intake of breath. Mrs. Blankenship said, "Oh!" faintly, her eyes widening. She recovered first.

"They did not," she said. "I'm sorry, Mr. King. Had I known, I would never have said that."

"But you believe it."

Her chin came up with the same patrician pride King had seen in the judge. "I do," she said.

"Thank you, ma'am. I came here to look up some things in the county records. Do you mind if I go ahead?"

The two women looked at each other. It was Mrs. Timm who answered.

"The office should be open at this hour. Cy would never want anyone who had business here turned away." She pressed her lips together, then nodded. "Very well. You can use that table over there. But nothing can be removed from the files."

"Thank you," King said. "It's been a pleasure to meet you both."

King first scanned through the land records for the southern part of Blackrock County, taking careful notes with a stub of pencil. Then he found the file on the inquest into the death of C.D. Hollis, County Sheriff. It didn't tell him much, nothing more than he'd already heard.

There were no eyewitnesses. Several people had heard the shots. The time was set pretty accurately by the passage of the westbound train. Felder gave a detailed description of the body, which King read twice, grimly. *People think it's buckshot does the work. But something smaller — say number four — does much more damage close up, it surely does.* Crow did not testify.

More quickly, he looked fhrough the file on Donny Castleberry's killing. It squared with what Felder had said, and offered nothing new. He returned the files to their shelves and left the office. The two women were still there, talking softly.

King climbed the stairs, found the judge's chambers, and rapped on the stout new wooden door. Judge Blankenship did not answer. King already knew the sheriff's office was locked. Apparently, both of them were still involved in looking for Timm. King tried to think where the little clerk might have gone, but gave it up. In any case, Timm's absence would worry the others. A quick check at Parnell and Son showed that the place was locked up, with Eli nowhere in sight. There must be a place I can stir things up a little, King thought. Maybe it's at the depot.

He walked down to the station. The train had pulled out, leaving a sleepy morning behind. King leaned over the counter and stared at Henry Drumm. "The thing is you put me in mind of somebody I've seen before."

Drumm grinned easily. "Yeah? Could be," he said. "My mother always thought I was the spitting image of U. S. Grant. That's why I grew the beard."

"I thought maybe it was to hide behind."

Henry Drumm's smile went flat. "Why would I want to do that?"

"Maybe because that face I remember was on a poster. Send me a telegram."

"To your mother?"

"Sure." King smiled. "Ask her to look on the wall for the picture of a man about forty. Dark brown hair going gray at the temples. Big round dark eyes like a rat's. Lots of big white teeth he can't keep his lips closed over."

"The hell —"

"Keep writing. Looks like the kind of rat that might come from New Mexico."

"By God —"

"Write! When she's checked that, she can look at the state land records for this county. My bet is she'll find something funny about the surveys in the southern townships. I want to know who has title and when they got it."

Drumm put down his pencil. "Write it up yourself," he said. "You've done gone past five dollars' worth, though."

"Five dollars? The hell with it. I'll handle this myself." He swung round and walked away, leaving Drumm to think about his future.

At the Hollis house, King called to the brown dog, gave him a strip of jerky, and went inside. He kindled a fire in one side of the kitchen stove.

Then he drew a pot of water for coffee and set it on to boil. He cut three big strips of bacon off the slab and laid them in a skillet. When he had turned the meat, he sliced off two thick pieces of bread and put them on top to warm and soak up the grease. It was ready by the time the coffee made.

He ate slowly, sitting there at a rickety table scorching his tongue with boiling coffee from a tin cup and fire-hot food off a tin plate. He figured he'd given Drumm enough to think about, and the other conspirators were out of reach for the moment. Timm's absence worried him. He was depending on Timm to be the first to crack, but that hadn't worked out. He thought again about joining in the search, then shook his head. He still had a promise to keep.

King washed his face, wiped his heavy little carbine clean, and went out onto the porch. The dog whined its question. "All right," King said, "come on."

In the hour after lunch, the Lost Mule was deserted except for a tall frail man behind the bar. He looked at King and the brown dog without enthusiasm.

"No dogs," he said in a voice like a frog in a well.

"That's all right. I don't need a dog. Already got one. Give me a whiskey — one shot, no more."

"We don't allow dogs."

King looked down at the brown dog. "Go home," he said. The dog ignored him, wagging its tail in slow, wide sweeps as it looked at the bartender. King shrugged. "You'd better talk to him. But first, I've waited a long while for this shot of whiskey, and I'm going to have it if I have to come get it myself."

Without another word, the tall man poured King a generous slug of whiskey. "I beg your pardon," he said with dignity. "I had not noticed it was that particular dog. He is a regular."

King thought about that. Then he drank off half the glass. "I thought the Crow kept this bar."

"He helps out. When he's sober. Which is not often."

"And today?"

"He went early on to dig a grave. He hasn't come back. It happens when he finds a bottle."

"Whose grave?"

"I don't know. He didn't know. He gets bad feelings, so he goes out and starts on a grave, just to be ready. Pretty soon, we get the word that someone has already died or is just now teetering on the edge." The barkeep rested his elbows on the polished wood and shook his head. "I've known Cuervo the better part of a dozen years. I have yet to see a grave he dug go to waste."

King drank off the rest of the whiskey. It was better than Crow's had been, but not much better. The barkeep roused himself and offered the bottle again, but King laid his hand over the glass. "No," he said, "that'll do. Thank you." He leaned across the bar near enough to smell the sourness of the host's breath. "Tell me something soft and quick."

"At your service, I'm sure. I'd rather hand out information than sell a drink most any time."

"I said *soft*. There is a woman called Maria Perez. I'd intended to ask Crow where to find her. Since I can't find him, I'm asking you."

The tall man passed a damp towel over the bar, leaving it shiny with moisture. "Don't take this in the wrong way," he murmured, "but if you're looking for entertainment, I think you'll be disappointed. If I might suggest another young lady —"

"I've found damn little entertainment any-where in this town," King interrupted. "Only Miss Perez will do. It is a personal matter, con-cerning a mutual friend. If you wouldn't mind, just tell me the way and I'll move along."

With a bony forefinger on the moist wood of the bar, Winkler lined off a likeness of the square, marked the Lost Mule, and drew a trail to a point King thought he could reach.

"There. But if you don't find what you're after, I'll still be here."

"Thank you," King said again. "I'll surely bear that in mind." He passed his palm over the map, smearing it into stray droplets of water. Then he laid a silver dollar on the bar and took up his carbine. "For your trouble. Maybe you'll forget my question."

"Question? Never been much good at remembering questions. Good luck."

King walked down to the livery stable and waited while the boy saddled his horse. The *jacal* where Maria Perez lived was half a mile or so from town, not far from the cemetery. King rode there slowly, circling back a couple of times to be certain he wasn't followed. At last he fetched up in front of a little adobe house. He tied the roan to a tall creosote bush, then cocked the carbine and tapped the door with its muzzle.

"Maria Perez," he said. "I bring word from the *Señora* Castleberry."

After a moment he heard a sound at the door, then a voice on the other side. "Yes?"

"She sent you a gift. I have it here for you."

"Leave it by the door," she said. "I am afraid."

"I have to talk with you first. Please let me in."

Within the house, a voice moaned sharply.

"Are you all right?"

"*Sí*. Go away."

"All right. I'm leaving the gift beside the door. Good evening." He stepped to one side and waited. He heard the moan again. Finally the door opened a bit. The brown dog put his nose in the crack and pushed his way inside the little house.

"Oh you!" Maria cried. "You rascal! Come here to Maria. Are you the gift!"

King opened the door and stepped inside the close little house. "No," he said.

Maria Perez looked about twenty. Her glossy black hair framed a heart-shaped face with a small chin and frightened brown eyes. She was some three or four months pregnant. She backed away from him to stand at the folds of a blanket dividing the tiny house into two rooms. The dog growled at King.

King held out the knotted handkerchief. "From the *señora,*" he said quietly. "You can see I want to help you."

For an answer the young woman brought a heavy pistol from beneath her shawl. Without cocking it, she pointed C.D. Hollis's Colt at King. The moan came again, louder, from the other side of the curtain. "Go away," Maria said.

King took one step, grabbed the gun away from her, and pointed the butt of it toward the growling dog. "If you ever growl at me again . . ." he said. But he didn't finish it. Instead he looked at the woman.

"Is it your husband in there, hurt?" he wanted to know.

"My husband!" she cried. "I have no husband, thanks to your kind." She reverted to Spanish to call him a name he understood and a couple he was glad not to know. But beyond the curtain, the moaning was louder than her insults.

King put a hand out toward the woman, thought better of touching her, and slid back the curtain instead. On a cot in the corner lay a dark, burly little man, the right side of his shirt soaked in blood.

"Crow!" King went to the cot, bent over it. "Crow with a broken wing," he muttered. Looking back at Maria, he pointed to the injured man. *"Mi amigo,"* he said.

Maria stared at him, uncertainty battling the hatred in her dark eyes. "They shot him," she said.

"Who shot him?"

She shrugged her shoulders and turned away. King again bent close to Cuervo, smelled a liquor he didn't know about, and looked at the arm. Then he cut away the stiffened sleeve and found the bullet wound.

"Where is the doctor?"

Maria Perez laughed. "If the doctor comes, they would know they haven't killed him!"

He understood. "I'll want some whiskey," he said, "or tequila — something like that. And your best knife. Bring the lamp over here. Is that all the wick it's got?"

Half an hour later he had done the best he could with the arm. Cuervo had not awakened. "Listen," King said to the woman. "You said they killed your husband."

"In God's eyes."

"You mean the same ones that did this?" He nodded toward the sleeping man. She shrugged her shoulders. "Didn't Cuervo tell you who shot him?" She shook her head. "All right," he told her. "I have to go now. I'll leave the dog with you, but you won't need the gun."

"I want it. I'm afraid."

"Sorry. It belonged to my brother. Do you have his notebook?"

She stared at him, her pretty face still and closed.

"His silver pen?"

She did not answer, but he saw that she knew what he meant. "Keep the door locked," he told her. "I'll be back." Then he went outside. He intended to put more wood in the stove to boil the stew pot, and he wanted to figure out why someone had shot Cuervo.

Chapter 24

December 7, 1894

Buck Parnell looked at his cards. A straight flush. It was the best hand he'd been dealt in a month or more. He was trying to figure how to get the bets up higher when the Mexican boy came up to tug at his shirtsleeve and whisper in his ear.

"Why hell," Buck said. "You *sure* it's a white man?"

"*Sí,*" said the visitor.

"And you found him *where?*"

"At the inn of the stagecoach on Rio Leon."

Buck slammed his fist down on the saloon table, startling the other players. Then he said, "We'll take this up when I get back." He put his cards in his shirt pocket. "With exactly the cards we're all holding now!"

"When you get back?" Hamilton Felder protested. "How are we supposed to know when that'll be?"

"I'll see it isn't long. And you might as well get ready. Sounds like he's bringing you some business."

"What's that?"

"Never mind." Buck drew a clasp knife from

his pocket, snapped it open with a jerk of his wrist, and pinned Felder's cards to the table. "Soon's we finish our official duties, we'll play out the hand just the way it sits."

He strode out of the Lost Mule with the boy. In the street, a slight and elderly Mexican man waited, holding the heads of a pair of slight and elderly horses attached to a rickety wagon.

"Where?" Buck asked.

"In the back."

The sheriif started around to one side, then stopped dead. Tied to the tailboard and fighting the rope was a tall black horse. Buck looked at the horse, then examined the saddle it still wore.

"Oh, hell," he breathed. Knowing what he was going to find, he turned his attention to the body giving shape to an old striped Indian blanket in the wagon's bed. Drawing back the blanket, he uncovered the face and chest of Cy Timm.

"God save us!" he said aloud. "Another shotgun." He looked quickly toward the corner of the courthouse where light was showing in the window of the judge's office, then turned his gaze on the old man. "Where did you find him? What's your part in this?"

"Ayah," said the old man. "*Nada, Señor!* We did nothing but to pick up the poor body and bring it here. The body and this curious thing which you will want to see because you are the law." He began searching within his serape.

"Just you take the body on down to that white building. No, the new one. *Nuevo. Blanco.* What

232

curious thing? What the hell is *that?*"

"It was lying on his vest — as if someone had placed it there for a sign."

"What do you mean? What kind of sign?"

"I know nothing, *señor*. But none like these, I think, do grow near that place."

"You get him on down to the funeral parlor. And don't you tell nobody else about it." Buck touched his badge with a heavy thumb. "Leave the signs to me, you hear?"

"*Bueno.* I shall know nothing about it."

"See that you don't."

"Mr. Sheriff?"

"What else is it?"

"These man's pistol. I put it in his pocket to keep it safe. It had been shot until no bullets were left."

Buck Parnell stared at the old man. "Cy had a gun?" he asked at last. He did not want to look at the body again. "Which pocket? You get it out and hand it to me."

Buck took the Colt and waved the wagon along toward Felder's place. Then he turned sharply and walked away across the street toward the courthouse. Someone was calling after him from the doorway of the Lost Mule, but it wasn't Felder. Felder was already hurrying toward his business, struggling into his coat and his solemnity as he went.

Buck Parnell had many things to think about, and he did not like to think very long at a time. He knew the pistol the old man had just handed him; he'd seen it often enough in the store. None of it made sense to him, least of all the small object he clutched in a sweaty hand. He went up the courthouse steps on the run. A moment later, breathing hard and shaking a little, he hove up in front of the judge's office and pounded on the door. Then he swore at himself for the formality and pushed his way inside. The judge was half-way around his desk, tugging at a small pistol which had caught by the hammer in his coat pocket.

"Judas, Judge! Look out where you're pointing that!"

"You made enough noise to — I thought you were —" Blankenship stopped and got hold of himself with a visible effort. "What's happened?"

"He's killed! Murdered! With a shotgun, just like Hollis!"

"Who's killed? Not King?"

"Cyril."

"What? No!"

"I'm telling you. Cy Timm. You want me to draw you a picture of a little man with the whole middle blowed out of him?"

"Hold your voice down! Shut the door at least. Who did it?"

Buck Parnell closed the door and locked it with the key. Striding forward, he laid his hand flatly on the judge's desk, then pulled it away to reveal a shiny black bean.

"Reckon the killer forgot to leave his name.

But he left this right on Cy's chest — what there was of it."

"Get hold of yourself, man. You're shaking."

"Well, by God! You come with me to the funeral parlor and I'll show you something to make *you* shake!"

"Just calm down. Here! Take a drink of this." Blankenship sloshed a small glass half full of brandy, handed it to his sheriff, and recorked the heavy French bottle. "I'd not expected you to lose your nerve."

"Hell," Buck said. "I ain't afraid of anybody I can see. But this —" He took the glass and he drank off the brandy. "Listen to me now. Can't you see? Somebody knows! And that somebody just killed one of us. You think that's the end of it?"

"No."

"Well it won't be! Next thing he'll do is kill one of the rest of us and then another one and then —"

"I understand the mathematics of it," Blankenship said. He jerked the cork out of the bottle and poured Buck another heavy shot. "I repeat, whom do you think did it?"

Parnell let the brandy burn a path all the way to his stomach. Then he put down the glass. His voice was steadier.

"It's somebody knew about the beans — somebody that was there, has to be — unless one of us talked." He looked sharply at Blankenship. "You and Cy did have kind of a little girls' fuss in the alley a night or two back. Seems to me you used the word bean."

"Damn you, sir! Who are you to be listening to gentlemen's private conversations?"

"That don't matter. I heard you. I've always thought you'd be the one for the rest of us to worry about. And you were mighty quick to grab that little hideout Smoot just now." Buck leaned across the judge's desk. "I want to hear you say you didn't kill poor Cy. And you better make me believe it."

"Take your hand off that gun, you fool. Of course I didn't kill Cy. Why would I? Who'd want to hurt Cy?"

"Don't ask me, damn it! And don't be calling me a fool, not ever again, or I'll put you through, so help me."

"Listen, you — listen, Buck. We're all of us best of friends. And besides, we're going to need every man we've got."

"Sure we are. What do you mean 'every man we got'?"

"It's a war when one side starts shooting."

"You mean Castleberry."

"Yes. And the Ranger. He was the one who first mentioned beans to Cyril. He knows."

Someone tried to open the door, then knocked quietly but urgently. Blankenship and Buck each had a gun in his hand immediately. "Yes," Blankenship said, "who is it?"

"Drumm."

The judge let him in. Before he could lock the

door again, Eli Parnell rushed breathlessly up the stairs and forced his way inside.

"Is it true? What are those guns for?" Eli demanded.

"Are you aiming to shoot somebody?" Drumm asked in the same moment. "Is that brandy? My God, I could use — Why are you playing with beans again? Odd man out? Drawing for me?"

"Don't be a —" Blankenship began, then broke off with a glance at Buck. "Go ahead. Have a drink, by all means. You two get drunk and go make idiots of yourselves all over town."

Drumm picked up the black bean. "Answer me about this. And answer damn quick."

"Put it down," the sheriff said. "It's evidence. Them Mexes that found Timm say it was on his chest, like it was left there."

Eli caught his breath. "Then it is true," he said. "Poor Cy! He'd been acting funny ever since King came. And it was me sold him that gun."

"Gun?" Buck turned to his older brother. "What the hell did he — ?"

"It's King," Drumm interrupted. He turned the bean over in his palm, stared at it, and then put it down. "We know it all, then, don't we?"

"What do we know?"

"That King killed him. He's come in the station two times or three ragging me — sending a telegram to Austin City like he's fixing to make arrests or he knows everything we've done."

"Hell, he's done the same with me," Buck said.

"That don't mean nothing."

"No? Last time he came in, he laid a black bean on the counter. This very one here, for all I know." Drumm shook his head. "It has to be him. He's got no real evidence for a jury, so he intends to murder us one by one."

"Not me, by God!"

"Sit down," the judge said. "Sit down, all of you. We must think this thing through and make a plan."

"Only plan's to find him and kill him!"

"Buck, no!" Eli put in. "Not that. There must be some other way."

"That's right," the judge agreed quickly. "Let's think a moment. I propose that Buck go straight to him and arrange a meeting between him and me."

"Why?"

"That's the right question. So that I can find out what he knows, and who else knows it." Blankenship sat back in his chair and frowned up at the skylight. "There's more here than we understand. I'll try to reason with him. If I should fail, you and Eli and Henry will be stationed in such a fashion as to prevent Mr. King from leaving."

Eli blinked. "Prevent him? Prevent him how?"

"He means by blowing his brains out," Drumm said with a grin.

"Hell, that's what *I* said to start with!"

"Should it come to that, we will do it with as little circus as possible."

"You mean be quiet about blowing his brains out."

Buck snorted. "Hell. He'll know it's a trap."

The judge nodded again. "Certainly," he said. "King's not a fool. He'll know."

"Then he won't come."

"Of course he will. Since the first moment he came here, he's been pushing, prying at us, trying to make one of us crack. When I ask to meet with him, he will be sure he's succeeded. As Henry said, if he can't find evidence, he'll hope we provide him an excuse to kill us."

"The way he did Cy," Drumm finished.

"Perhaps."

"Perhaps, hell."

"Gentlemen. If it comes to killing, we will place the body on Castleberry's land in such a way that he will be incriminated beyond denial."

"Those of us that's still alive, you mean."

"Yes." Blankenship nodded slowly. "There's that." He looked at the others, one by one. "This time, we cannot make do with beans and secrecy. We must act together, or we're likely to die separately."

"I'm in."

"Me too."

"Oh, God. God help us. We have to do it."

Blankenship nodded. "Sit down, gentlemen, while I make some coffee. We'll settle our nerves and plan our campaign. When we're ready, Buck can go fetch Mr. King."

Chapter 25

December 7–8, 1894

Hamilton Felder had not yet stripped Cyril Timm's body when someone tapped at his workroom door. He pulled a curtain across the embalming area, and opened the door. "Good evening," Felder said. "I thought you'd be the sheriff, but apparently no one's been able to find him yet. They surely haven't. I guess they found you instead."

"No one found me," Jeff King said. "I heard bells. I saw a wagon come by. Then I saw it in front of your parlor. Has there been a death?"

"I'm afraid that we've lost our county clerk, Cyril Timm."

"How did he die?"

"I haven't gotten very far with the remains, but I'd certainly say he died by gunshot."

"Gunshot?"

"Shotgun."

"Like Sheriff Hollis?"

"Well." Decorum slowed the undertaker's response. "I would guess the difference to be —"

"Was it the same gun?"

"I couldn't tell a thing like that."

"You were going to say the difference was — what?"

"A matter of quantity. I'm afraid Mr. Timm got both barrels."

King stood for a moment in silence. Then, reluctantly, he said, "I'll need to see him."

Felder wasn't sure. "Well. I guess maybe it's a county matter. Perhaps we should wait for the sheriff."

"Don't make me press the matter of jurisdiction."

"I take your point, I surely do. This way, please."

It was worse than King had expected. He remembered from the transcript of the inquest on Hollie's death the dry, precise phrases describing the body. Here was that description written in shredded bits of cloth and bone fragments and torn flesh. Hardened as he was to the sight of dead and wounded men, King turned away white and shaken.

"I'm sorry," Felder said.

"Hollie. He was — like this?"

The undertaker nodded. "Pretty much. Only one barrel, as I said, but the shot was smaller. The effect of that —"

"I understand."

"Yes."

Felder hesitated, seeming to want to say more. Then they both heard the outer door open and close. "Mr. Felder?" a woman's voice called. "Mr. Felder, are you here?"

"That's Mattie. Mrs. Timm," Felder said. "The widow," he added in a different tone.

"She must have heard the church bells, too."

Felder looked at him strangely. "No," he said. "Those bells are for Emma Castleberry." He glanced at the closed door. "Cy — the body — isn't ready for — viewing. Could you — ?"

"All right."

"Oh, Mr. King!" Mattie Timm hadn't taken time to make her face or brush her hair. One stocking had fallen to her ankle. Her long coat was buttoned unevenly. "I've heard rumors. Terrible rumors about Mr. Timm's absence. Can you tell me the truth?"

Jeff King came to the tall woman and took her by the arm. He shook his head. "I'm sorry," he said, "but Mr. Timm is gone. He was shot — murdered." He held on to her arm, waiting for her to scream or fight or faint.

"I never doubted it," she said. "Nothing else in this world would have made him miss lunch a second time." The wildness ebbed out of her eyes. "I want to see him."

"After a while. Mr. Felder is with him now." He moved her toward the visitors' couch. "Won't you sit here?"

She sat. "Will you wait with me, Mr. King? It would be a great help to me, you being a professional man like Mr. Timm."

King sat on the couch. He knew Cyril Timm had plotted to kill C.D. Hollis. He had suspected him of being the murderer, and was sure he'd written the letter that called the Rangers in. Given any definite evidence to act on, King might very easily have killed Timm himself. Instead he was trying to comfort Timm's widow. "Yes," he said, "of course."

"I never doubted it," she said again, softly.

"Pardon?"

"Mr. Timm was such a strong and forceful man — stubborn, too, I suppose. I was so concerned that something like this would happen. I told him to be careful, but of course, he wasn't afraid."

"Of course," King murmured, trying to match the Timm she'd known to the one he had met. He gave it up and said, "Do you have any idea who might have wanted to kill him?"

She looked at him in surprise. "Why, of course. He was involved in a business venture with Judge Blankenship and the Parnell brothers — I think Henry Drumm, too. They had made enemies — you know how it is in business — of your brother and Dallas Castleberry." She shook her head. "I did not know Sheriff Hollis well, but Dallas Castleberry is a hard and vengeful man. It would not surprise me if he were at the bottom of this."

King said, "I see. How about Mr. Timm's business partners?"

"Oh, no. I hardly think any of them would have dared to cross Mr. Timm." She looked at him with a faint smile. "Of course, he did say that *you* might try to kill him. But I do not believe that of you."

"Thank you." King took a paper from his coat pocket and spread it open before her. "One more question, if you will. Is this your husband's handwriting?"

Mattie Timm drew a pair of bow-rimmed spectacles from her bosom and squinted through them at the letter. "Oh, no," she said. "This is nothing like Cy's. He wrote a beautiful hand." She looked up at him. "Don't you remember? He copied out those documents you read in his office."

King closed his eyes for a moment, picturing the firm, round signature at the bottom of the inquest report: *Sworn and attested, Cyril P. Timm, County Clerk.* That picture gave way to another, a sweeping panorama of his own stupidity.

"Thank you, ma'am."

"Why? Was that important?"

"Yes, ma'am."

The door from the workroom opened and Hamilton Felder slipped through. He had shed his gloves and apron in favor of a gray frock coat and a somber expression.

"Mattie, we're ready now," he intoned softly.

Mattie Timm rose, very straight and tall. "Thank you. Good evening, Mr King."

"Ma'am."

Jeff King left the mortuary with a renewed respect for shotguns and none at all for his own good sense. The last thing he had wanted was another murder to solve. He did not like it at all that the victim had been one of his suspects in the murder of his brother.

He especially did not like it now that he knew Cyril Timm certainly had not written the letter. If not Timm, then who? Someone had killed poor Timm, maybe to keep him quiet. That same someone might have shot Crow as well. But King seemed not one inch closer to knowing why, let alone to finding C.D.'s killer. Something ugly and explosive was going on in Blackrock County, and King was doing a pitiful job of stopping it.

Taller than anything except the new courthouse, the distant church bell tower still was singing. God in heaven, King thought. He had forgotten all about Emma Castleberry. And Diana, who had lost her mother.

King remembered how that was — cocoa, games beside the fireplace, wine-colored carpet with big flowers, and then two white coffins in the parlor. *We'll have to take care of each other, Jeff Davis. That's what brothers do.* It was different for Diana, of course. She was a woman, not a child. But even so, King hesitated, wondering. Where did his first duty lie — in comforting the only woman he had ever cared for right to the bone, or in finding his brother's killer?

He'd barely taken two more steps before he almost walked smack into Sheriff Buck Parnell. He let his hand fall on one of his pistols.

"Why hell," Parnell said, smiling. "And you the very one I was looking for."

It seemed to King that the sheriff had not been looking very carefully. But then neither had he. "Why hell," he said.

"No, now listen. I've got a message from Judge Blankenship. We think — he thinks you all can clear up this whole matter of Hollis's death. Just wants to talk it over with you."

"He the only one wants to talk?"

"Why hell, sure. I mean me and Drumm and Eli — we'll be out of the way. It'll be just you and the judge."

King was thinking about it. "When?" he said.

"Tomorrow night. About midnight, so's not too many people know about it. Out at Leon Creek, the old stage station."

King liked it. Now that Timm was gone, King would never prove that the little gang of them killed Hollis. He'd even have trouble tying them to the land grab business. But something was making them nervous enough to force their hand.

"All right. But not out there. The judge wouldn't be comfortable."

"Why hell."

"He'll be more comfortable in his own office."

"I'll have to talk to him about that," Parnell said. But the thought produced the edges of a grin. "I'll let you know."

King never doubted that the others would be around in the shadows. He didn't care. He'd worked hard to shake them up. Now that he'd done it, he was ready for a showdown with them. C.D. had said he'd know who to hang if he had a rope, but evidence was harder to come by. If King hadn't liked that idea before, he understood it now. Let the judge or any one of them cock a hammer at him, he would kill them all right down to the last button. "Do that," he said. "I'll be there."

Early the next morning, he took the road to the DC. His boots were blacked and his coat brushed. He wore no gun belt, but his .45 rode heavily in his coat pocket. Save for a single sentry, the ranch headquarters was deserted. King heard the tolling of a distant bell. From its tone, he thought it must be silver.

All the way up the curving white road to the hilltop he'd visited with Diana, he held his horse to a slow walk. At the top, he tied it to the first low tree and walked the rest of the way to the tiny chapel from which the congregation was overflowing. A pump organ filled the small cathedral with the melody of a hymn King didn't recognize. He saw two dozen souls standing outside in their shining best and moved into the edge of the group.

There he found the saddler Constanzo Alvarez sweating in his best woolen suit. They shook hands, nodded silently in deference to the music, looked away. King heard parts of the liturgy but understood almost none of the clerical Latin.

He could see that Alvarez didn't understand it either. King leaned close to him and spoke softly in his ear. "When did this happen? When did she pass away?"

"One night ago," the saddler said. "A very sad

thing. Until the death of her son, she was a strong woman. After that . . ." He shrugged and rolled his eyes.

King nodded. "A sad thing," he whispered. "On the other hand, there are the two ponies." King looked at him.

"That is a happy thing," Alvarez explained. His brown face creased in a smile. "They grow fat from having no one to ride them and train them. And the saddles also are ready!"

An elderly Mexican woman shot a look at Alvarez that quieted him. Then she looked at and through King and turned her face back toward the chapel. Feeling unwelcome, he edged nearer the door again, trying to hear the service. Once he heard the deceased's name. Finally the young priest switched to English for a brief eulogy for a woman who must have been very special.

From time to time he heard a low keening from the women; then at last the priest came down the aisle and out the door moving slowly so that the pallbearers with their burden could keep pace. Saul and Octavio led the way, the older man's face wet with tears. King stepped clear of their path. The vaqueros strode past without a glance of recognition. Dressed in their finest colors, immersed in their ritual of mourning, they moved in a different world from King, one that did not include him.

He felt it and wanted to be a part of that world, but knew in that moment that he was an outsider. No matter what happened, no matter if he and

Diana loved and married and lived there a hundred years, he would always be an outsider on the DC.

Then the family emerged from the chapel door, Castleberry, Diana, and Socorro, who moved as though she were part of them. Glistening in black from head to toe. Leather polished. Fine black material brushed or new. Black eyes glowing.

Diana saw King, let her eyes rest on him for a troubled moment. Castleberry and the others about him did not see King at all. He realized he should have stayed in town where he had a brother dead and a job to do finding his killers. Instead he had come out to the funeral of a woman he didn't know for the benefit of people who didn't want to remember him.

He followed at a distance as the rest crowded behind the family into the fenced cemetery where a dark mound of earth marked a new grave. More words were pronounced. Earth was tossed. Prayers were spoken. At last the congregation parted to let the family pass along toward the iron gate. Jeff King stood fifty feet away at the corner of the low fence and watched first the family and then the larger group trickle out of the cemetery and trail down the hill to the headquarters.

Three or four men remained at the grave. King stepped over the fence and walked slowly to them. One wore a cassock and introduced himself as the priest. King shook hands with him. Then he interrupted the workers to shake hands with them. Their grips were limp and uninterested. Without looking at King directly, they went back to work filling the grave.

Bridging the someday-two graves stood the enormous stone King had seen before. The names were unchanged, *Dallas Castleberry* and *Emma Castleberry* but a pair of dates and another line of script had been added below the second: *1838–1894 Asleep in the Lord.*

In some sense of courtesy, King led his horse back down the hill, intending to walk it past the house before he got back in the saddle and headed for Willow Springs where he had more pressing business. But then the saddler called out *"Señor"* and King turned toward the smaller barn. He wanted to see a friendly face before he left the DC.

Alvarez showed him the saddles, pointed out the window to the ponies frolicking in the pasture behind the house. "I was told to wonder," the man said, "when you would want to take them with you." He looked hopefully at his visitor.

King did not smile. "Costs that much to feed them, does it?" He saw that he was an outsider to all these people, that they all wanted him to leave. He wasn't comforted by the realization that a few days earlier he had been more eager to leave than they would ever be to see him go.

"Feed?" The saddler did not understand.

"All right. Tomorrow. The day after. No later than that. If they're that much in the way, I'll take them with me now."

"Constanzo didn't mean no offense." The familiar voice came from the door behind King. "I told him to ask you."

He turned slowly to look at Dallas Castleberry. The rancher looked taller, more gaunt than King remembered. "No offense taken," he said. "I came to offer my condolences. I was almighty sorry to hear of your wife's passing."

"Obliged," Castleberry said. "You were here. She was gone when I carried her up the stairs." He cleared his throat. "You about got the rest of your killers rounded up?"

King hadn't been imagining it. Everybody wanted him gone. "Rest of them?" he asked.

"Heard you got one of them. Timm."

"*I* didn't get him."

"Hm. Maybe they'll kill each other off till there's only one left. Then you can arrest him."

"I have a meeting with them tonight," King said. "I'll take care of it."

"Meeting? Ambush, more likely. Best you go shooting."

"I'll talk if I can. Two or three questions I'd still like answered. I'll shoot if I have to."

"Suit yourself. Reckon you're done seeing the saddles. Come up to the house if you like."

"Kind of you," King said. "I'll be getting back to my work."

"Diana'll expect you," the rancher said. "But likely you know best. Not everybody's meant for an outfit like the DC."

King walked past him to the rail where he'd

tied the roan. "We'll talk about that later," he said. "After the work's done."

When Jeff King started up the south end of Main Street toward the square, he saw Sheriff Buck Parnell on horseback heading west from the courthouse. King nudged his horse to a trot, cut off to his left to go round the square past Maria's shack and up the old cemetery road he had never taken. Then he stopped. Two hundred yards down the way, Parnell rode through the main cemetery gate, stopped for a moment at an open grave, and went straight on along the narrow grass road toward the back.

King followed through the gate, came to a shallow unfinished grave, and saw Buck's horse standing untended in a far corner. It made no sense. King dismounted and walked on toward a shed he had not seen before. Inside it, judging from the noise, a clumsy army was playing catch with wash tubs.

The broken door stood open. King went to it and looked in. Buck Parnell was bending over the shattered pieces of a workbench. "Why hell," King said, "was it termites, or mice?"

Parnell straightened as quickly as a young Indian brave, a bright nickel pistol in his hand and a savage ragged grin on his face. "You know damned well what I'm looking for, friend," he said. "You're the one put me on to it."

King did not understand. "No," he said. "Whose grave is that next to the road?"

"Could be yours."

"Or yours. Or Timm's. But I only asked you —"

"Why hell! I guess it *is* Timm's. That crazy old man always starts a grave day or two before somebody dies. The devil tells him when it's time. And he's the devil I was looking for, if it's any of your concern."

"Crow?"

"Sure." Parnell put his gun back in its leather.

"You figure him to be hiding under that bench?"

"Why hell."

King pulled a common but badly misshapen lead bullet out of his coat pocket and pitched it to Parnell who caught it out of habit. "Of course it could be he was digging that grave for himself, knowing that somebody was fixing to shoot him with a forty-five pistol."

Caught for the moment with no ready words, Buck Parnell reached again for his gun. King grabbed the brand-new shovel handle at his elbow and swung the hickory hard against the side of Parnell's head, catching him across the left ear and felling him like an ox on the slaughterhouse floor. King threw down the broken half of the stick with the thought that it was a poor use of a good handle.

When he was certain that Parnell was in no shape to follow him, King rode back down the outlying lane to Maria's little house. The smile on her face when she opened the door to him was the best moment he'd had all day. The brown dog woofed and wagged his tail.

Over in his corner, Cuervo coughed with a vigor that suggested he was stronger. King drew back the curtain and grinned at the grave digger. "How's your wing?"

Cuervo peered at him brightly. "Can't fly for a while."

"Neither can the one that likely shot you. Did you see him?"

Crow shook his head. "Not a thing, no, just glints and noises and then I was in that hole, cah-hawf! Reckon some folks must've come along, so's he couldn't come and finish poor Crow." He made a sad and solemn face, but his black eye was fixed on the shiny nickel-plated pistol in King's belt. "Caw?" he murmured.

King drew out the pistol and held it out butt first to Cuervo who couldn't move far enough to grasp it. "I brought this to trade."

"Caw-cawf? Trade? What's old Crow got to trade?"

"For Hollis's notebook."

Maria brought him a cup of something like tea. *"Momentito,"* she said quietly. When she returned she had a leather notebook in one hand and a silver fountain pen in the other.

He accepted them, then gave the pen back to her. "No," he said. "I want you to have the pen."

"No. I want nothing of his, for what he did to my Donny!"

Slowly, King put the pen in his pocket. "Ever

fired a shotgun?" he asked.

"*No sabe.*"

King repeated the question in Spanish. Maria stared at him, then shook her head violently.

"No. I would have killed him. But I did not, for the sake of . . ." She touched her rounded belly, flushed, and turned away, drawing her shawl across her face. "I did not. The lady Diana can tell you."

"I'm sorry." The words sounded flat and insincere. King was trying to better them when someone knocked at the door. Maria broke off to peek through a crack. Then she reached for the latch.

"Wait!" King said sharply. He was thinking that Parnell might have followed him after all.

But the door was already open, the visitor already rushing inside. "I saw your horse or I'd never have found you!" Diana cried. Then she flung into King's arms and held herself against him as if she were drowning.

Maria bent to look in both directions along the road. Then she bolted the door and turned her warm smile on the entwined couple before her. King had not seen anyone so happy since he could remember. "Here," she said brightly. She swept things off a little sofa and bade them sit on it. Then she turned away to her own corner of the room.

At first, they did not sit. Diana did not even seem aware of furniture or people or house. "Jeff," she said.

"Yes." He murmured it into her hair.

"I want to go away with you."

"What?"

That unsettled her. She tilted her head back to look up at him. "If you want me."

He held her. "Oh yes," he said finally.

"Now."

"Yes."

"Let's go *now*. Right this minute. Please, Jeff."

"Diana." The temptation rose in him, sharp and strong. *Where did his first duty lie?* "It's not over."

"It has to end somewhere." Diana might have read his thoughts. "Let it end here — with us. You won't bring your brother back by hunting down — who? — someone. Stop now, Jeff, before —" She gulped, fought back a sob. "— before you spoil it all."

King frowned. Dallas Castleberry had said almost the same thing, days before. "It won't spoil things for us," he said, "no matter what I find out. But I can't stop." He hesitated, then said, "Could you? If it was Donny?"

"That's not the same!" Then she covered her face again. "But it is, isn't it? No. You won't stop. I see that."

"Will you wait until I'm done?"

She raised overflowing dark eyes to his, her hands clasped as though in prayer. "Ask me then," she said. "When you're done, ask me then."

Chapter 26

December 8, 1894

"My God, man, what's happened to you?" Blankenship demanded.

"Buck! Are you all right?" Eli Parnell said at the same moment.

"Never mind about me." Buck spoke thickly and with difficulty. A blue bruise ran along his left cheekbone and back into his hair. His left eye was swelled almost closed, his ear purple and puffy with trapped blood. "Just never mind me. It's King. He'll meet with you, all right, and I'll kill the son of a bitch myself."

They were in the judge's chambers, the judge in his usual place behind the big desk. The lamps were not burning, but gray afternoon light streamed through the big iron-framed skylight. Henry Drumm perched on the edge of the desk like a cat in the sunshine, stroking his fingers through his brown beard. Eli stood like a wooden statue in the corner of the room next to the massive bookcase. Judge Blankenship leaned back in his carved chair and steepled his hands, looking at Buck.

"Very well. But according to our plan."

"To hell with your plan."

"Buck!" Eli said. "Be still."

Buck turned on him, fists balled. Then he caught hold of himself and drew back. "He'll come," he said. "But not where you wanted him, Judge. Right here, he said. Right here in your little hidey-hole at midnight."

Blankenship stared at him for a moment. Then, surprisingly, he laughed. "Well, Mr. King has more of a sense of fitness than I would have expected. That will be excellent."

"Will it?" Drumm stirred, frowning. "We'll have to forget about putting the killing onto Castleberry. If we start shooting at the court-house, there's no hiding it."

Blankenship nodded slowly. "Yes. We must change our plans, but it can't be helped. We'll act openly if we must, in defense of our lives. No Willow Springs jury will dispute that."

"God's truth, too, if he's the one killed Cy," Eli put in.

"If?" Drumm snorted. "Who do you think killed Cy? The whole town's talking about it."

"So much the better for us." Blankenship looked slowly from one the other. "Gentlemen, are we agreed?"

When no one answered, Blankenship nodded again. "Very well. I'll meet him in chambers. The rest of you will stay back until he's inside, then close in."

"Why hell, Judge, that puts you in a tight spot. You figure he'll have a little chat with you, then just walk out where we can shoot him?" Buck laughed. "More likely, he'll kill you first. Better let us lay for him on the way in."

"No. We may be wrong about Cy. And King may be wrong about us. I'll talk to him and take my chances." Blankenship smiled thinly. "At least, I'll know he's not carrying a shotgun."

"I'm with Buck," Drumm said. "We've got to kill him — unless we all want to end up like Cy."

"No!" Eli cried. "Killing a Ranger's bad business, even if he doesn't get us instead. We mustn't risk it unless there's no other way."

"Scared, big brother?"

"Of course I'm scared. But I'll play to Homer's lead, whichever way it goes. And you'll do the same."

"Listen, just talking might not get it done. There's Hollis's notebook."

"What's that?"

"The notebook that bastard kept of everything he did. I tried to get it as soon as I found out, but it got away from me. If King has it, he'll use it to hang us."

"Buck!" Eli came toward him. "Why didn't you tell us this? What — ?"

"Just another reason to talk," Blankenship cut in impatiently. "If that notebook is around, I must find out where it is and what it contains." He rapped his knuckles on the desk unconsciously as if they were a gavel. "Now stop this bickering and listen. We'll do it this way. He will come to my chambers to talk. As soon as he's inside, Henry will take station in the second floor hallway. Buck, you stay on the ground floor where you can cover the stairs. Eli will wait outside in case he gets by us all. Take no chances. Again, I recommend shotguns."

Drumm rose abruptly. "Damn right, after what he did to Cy!" he said.

"Not me." Buck shook his head. "Not with a shotgun."

"It's more certain."

"Maybe so, but I won't do it. I've seen too much of that." He slapped the pistol at his hip, nickel-plated and shiny like its confiscated mate. "Don't worry, I can stop him with this. I owe him a little something."

"Perhaps. But remember, we fight only if we must. If we can end this without more killing, that is the course we will follow."

No one argued. But as they filed out, Drumm caught Buck's eye and grinned tightly, slowly drawing the tip of his forefinger across his throat. Buck laughed, startling Eli who was ahead of him, and inclined his head in perfect agreement.

Chapter 27

December 8, 1894

Jeff King stepped from the shadows of the alley into the darker shadow at the southeast corner of the square. He was early. Along the railroad tracks a quarter mile behind him, the screech and rumble of the eastbound express covered any sound he might make. Coming in from the south, he had passed the westbound train waiting on the siding and had satisfied himself that Drumm was not in his place at the depot. Now he settled into his dark corner, his back to a wall, and peered outward.

He had picked the spot carefully before dark. From there, he could see most of the square and parts of three sides of the courthouse. He knew that Buck and Drumm and probably even Eli were somewhere in the dark watching for him. Buck, at least, would be more than ready to kill him if that was their plan.

If they were on the square, he couldn't see them. Around on the far side, the Lost Mule was doing its Saturday night business, but his side of the square was quiet. Thin moonlight showed through a haze of clouds and a single bright star of the Dipper hung over the courthouse cupola. King waited, motionless, shivering a little in the cold wind that came across the valley floor — a little from the tension, too. In daylight, this confrontation had seemed a fine idea, the logical end to all the pressure he'd put on the conspirators. In the cold darkness of a December night, he wasn't quite so certain.

Halfway along one street, light shone beneath the side door of Higginbotham's store. Watching the shadows, King went along the boardwalk, listened a moment, and then tapped at the door. The shade moved enough for a gnat to peek past. King heard a key turning in the lock. Then the door opened far enough for the gnat to escape. "You alone?" Higginbotham wanted to know.

"Pretty much."

Higginbotham let him in and locked the door behind him. "Kinda late to be buying grub."

King looked at the heavy books stacked on the table and the sheets of paper covered with Higginbotham's painful writing that spread across the butcher's counter.

"Kinda late to be doing your accounts."

"Ain't." Higginbotham pressed his lips together as if upset that the word had escaped. He moved to the table and closed the one book that was open there. "Just doing some reading. Just for amusement."

King reached out and took the big leather-bound volume from the butcher's reluctant hand. *"Annotated Statutes of the State of Texas,"* he read aloud. "Pretty serious reading just for amusement."

The butcher scowled. "I'm the one been grousing about how this town's run," he said. "You're the one asked why I didn't do something about it." He snatched the book back. "Well, all right. But ain't all of us do their thinking with a gun, you know."

"I know." King laid his carbine on the counter and grinned. "Might be I've got some thinking to do tonight, though." He brought the leather notebook out of his coat. "I'll need some wrapping paper and string, I reckon."

"Why?"

"To mail it. Nothing much in it that a jury will buy, but if anything happens, I don't want it lost."

"Give it to me. Your hands are too clumsy for this kind of work." Higginbotham tore off a piece of butcher paper, wrapped the notebook tight and neat, and tied up the parcel like a trussed turkey.

King addressed the package and gave Higginbotham money to mail it. The butcher squinted at the address.

"To yourself?"

"Care of Captain Slater in Austin City," King confirmed. "I'll have it to look forward to when I get home for Christmas."

At half past eleven, King walked across the darkest part of Palisade Street into the shadow of an elm on the courthouse lawn. Then he went straight to the building, waited for his eyes to get used to the greater darkness, and started around the south side. He stayed within arm's reach of the wall. Close to the southeast corner he almost walked into a darker part of the darkness. He put out a hand and touched the cold black iron of the fire escape ladder.

At a better moment, he might have smiled at himself for being spooked by a ladder. Instead, he stepped out from the wall, strode through the faint field of light at the corner and climbed the outside stone steps to the second floor entrance. The big door was unlocked.

Thirty feet along the side hall a lamp shed its yellow light down the inside wooden stairs from the landing. King went to it like a reluctant moth, paused on the landing to look out a window onto the south lawn where he had been a moment earlier. Nothing moved. He went on up the stairs to the third floor. Brighter light shone through the open door at Judge Blankenship's chambers.

The situation did not look dangerous. It appeared to be just what it promised — a quiet, private, peaceful talk with the judge of Blackrock County. King made plenty of noise walking so that his host would hear him coming. Somewhere back down in the dark bowels of the building a bolt shot home to seal the big outside door behind him. As if in answer to a question, King nodded. Now he knew for certain. He tapped gently at the judge's door with the barrel of his carbine. When the judge answered, King cautiously pushed the door open and stepped inside.

"Welcome, welcome," Judge Blankenship said warmly. He was seated at the desk under the green-shaded hanging lamp, his hands spread flat and empty on the polished wood. "Don't worry about that little noise. I assure you we are alone so that we can speak frankly. As I can tell you from my many evenings here alone, a building this size creaks and snaps all night long. Sometimes I'd swear it screams! But never you mind that sort of thing. Come in, come in!"

Jeff King walked into the warmly paneled room, took off his hat, and shook hands with the anxious judge. "Makes noises, does it?"

"Oh yes. Here, hang your hat. Look around if you want to — that's a closet in there. Have a seat. Here. Well, all right, over there's fine too."

Blankenship rose to close the door, then crossed the room to his leather chair. He was neatly dressed in his suit and frock coat and seemed quite relaxed except for the shine of sweat on his forehead.

King took a chair at the far side of the judge's desk, away from the door. He rested the carbine across his lap and rested his thumb on its hammer. "How well does the sound carry in this building when somebody touches off a gun inside it?"

The judge stared at King. "All too well. Large rooms, tall ceilings. Sounds echo, you know. Yes, I heard the shots when your brother was killed.

I was sitting right here at this desk as I am now."

"That would take you out of suspicion, wouldn't it?"

"Yes. Decidedly. If you should choose to believe me. The first shot was a heavy thump. After maybe a count there was a second shot, sharper, more defined."

"What?"

"The third shot, which I now assume to be the second shotgun blast, was the loudest of them all. But then, the window would have been gone. And the last two shots were so close together that they made something like one big boom echoing off one another."

"You make it sound like poetry."

"Do I? It's from telling and retelling the story, then. I ran down to the sheriff's office. What I found was not at all poetic."

"How did you know where to run down to?"

Blankenship looked at his visitor with greater respect. Then he smiled a bit. "The sound made it clear enough. Down on the second floor the gunsmoke made it obvious."

"If you didn't do the shooting, which one of you did?"

"What do you imply?"

"I imply that you and your four friends planned Sheriff Hollis's death, that you drew lots — beans — to see which one of you would do the shooting."

"To what four friends do you —"

"Drumm, the Parnells, and Timm."

"And you killed poor Cyril Timm on no better evidence than that?"

"Killed him!" It was King's turn to stare. "Me? You think I did that?"

Blankenship sat back in his chair and smiled thinly. He was very careful to keep his hands in sight and to make his movements slow and deliberate.

"Let us say I suspect it," he said. "Buck and Henry Drumm are quite sure of it. Of course, it did occur to me that you might by some process of elimination be judging the township yourself."

"I've been tempted. But I don't own a shotgun. Looks to me like somebody in your little group's started weeding out the ones that might turn state's evidence."

"Yes." Blankenship steepled his hands and gazed thoughtfully at King. "I can see how you might think that — if you are being truthful with me. And I assume you think me the logical candidate."

"I do."

"I assure you that you are mistaken."

King shrugged. "You've put your finger on it. How can we trust one another? You've got the others waiting out there somewhere to kill me right now."

Blankenship folded his hands and considered King for what seemed a long time. Finally, he sighed. "I think I will decide to believe you, Mr. King. You have no reason to lie about Cy's death at this point. Given that, maybe I can convince you to believe me."

"You can try."

"We did draw lots to kill Sheriff Hollis. One of our number drew the black bean, but the plan wasn't followed. Hollis was killed that very night, before we were ready."

"What did you have against Hollis?"

"He blamed us for Donny Castleberry's death. He thought we had put him in position to kill the boy." Blankenship glanced sharply at King. "I assume his notebook told you as much — but you might have trouble proving our involvement."

"Maybe I don't need to prove it."

"I think you do." Blankenship smiled, seeming more at ease. "If you didn't murder Timm, it's unlikely you'll murder me. If you did . . ." He spread his hands. "As you say, the others are waiting outside."

King thought about it. Blankenship was either truthful or incredibly smooth. But he might also be wrong.

"I still think one of you killed Timm," King said. "Maybe not you, but one of your friends. The same one that wrote this letter." He drew an envelope from his pocket. "It had to be one of you — and whoever it is, he means to kill off the rest of you." He handed the envelope across to Blankenship. "I'll let you tell me. Did you write this?"

"No," the judge said immediately. Then he

took out his glasses and unfolded the letter, his face going white as he read. "My God," he said softly. "How . . . ?" He looked wide-eyed at King. "Not me, nor Cy. Not any of the others — I know their writing. But how could anyone else —"

He broke off abruptly. Raising his head, he stared upward past the lamp at the heavy iron-framed skylight. A faint sound, the clink of something against glass, came from that direction. Blankenship's face changed. He sprang up and snatched at his coat pocket.

"King, look out!"

King was already twisting away, thumbing back the carbine's hammer and swinging the weapon up toward the judge. But Blankenship didn't even glance his way. He was bringing up a small pocket pistol, face still turned upward, his mouth twisted with rage.

"You! You did —"

The green-shaded lamp exploded in flame and smoke and a hail of steel and glass fragments. Something — something more than glass and fragments — struck the carbine from King's right hand and lanced burning pain from his wrist to his shoulder. The shotgun blast filled the office with noise, and the concussion of it seemed to crush King into himself. He dived under the end of the desk, reached for his gun with a hand that wouldn't do what he expected of it, and rolled to look upward.

In the sudden darkness of the office, flame-streaked by patches of burning kerosene from the lamp, he saw Blankenship's pistol flare, once and then again, aimed upward at the gaping emptiness where the side of the skylight had been. Then the shotgun's second barrel boomed. The charge of shot took Blankenship in the belly, slammed him backward over his chair, broke him in two, splattered King with his blood. King found Hollis's gun in his belt, dragged it out left-handed, and angled a couple of shots up toward the skylight.

He heard the smack of his second bullet stopping short, heard a grunt, saw the quick glint of light on the barrels of a shotgun that fell through the hole in the ceiling to clatter heavily on the office floor. Footsteps rattled the roof as the man moved off along to the southeast. King didn't know which of the three conspirators might have been on the roof, nor why he would have shot the judge. For that matter, King thought, he couldn't imagine why the judge had tried to warn him. He was still puzzling that over when he found his handkerchief and got it wrapped around his right hand and wrist.

There were two or three other bad spots on his coat sleeve all the way to the elbow. He would have to worry about that a little later when he was done with — with whom? Of course it wouldn't have been one of the conspirators that shot the judge. No, it was someone else — someone who'd heard their plotting from above and sent the letter. Someone who'd killed C.D. Hollis. Someone who was getting away again.

He clambered to his feet, swaying and unsteady. There were some ragged spots on his pants leg too. He gritted his teeth and fumbled at his belt with clumsy fingers, trying to reload his pistol. With his left hand he couldn't do it anytime soon. He stepped over the shotgun, limped down the short inner hall to the door, and opened it wide.

Immediately a voice challenged him. "That you, Judge?" Henry Drumm sang out. He was somewhere down the hall and lower. King figured he must be at the landing on his way up the stairs.

"No," King said, "Listen, the one we want — the one that killed the judge — he's getting away." He started through the door.

"Like hell he is," Drumm said. The stairwell lit up with the flame from his shotgun muzzle just as King dived across the hall. Behind him the splinters of fine new wood scattered themselves along the corridor.

King hit the far wall with a shock that sent waves of agony through his whole right side. Below him, he heard Drumm thumb back the other hammer as he started up the stairs. "You'd tell them about New Mexico, would you?" Drumm said. "Well, now I don't think you'll be telling them nothing no more."

Bright lights danced in front of King and he squeezed his eyes shut to block them out. When he looked again, everything was dark as before and heavy footsteps were sounding on the stairs. King lay on his belly watching the top of the stairway as he slid his left arm up to point in that direction. Right then he would have given Henry Drumm amnesty and fifty dollars just to get out of his way. But Drumm wasn't having any of it. King let him come up the stairs until his head showed above the hall floor. Then, before Drumm's eyes accustomed themselves to the darkness along the floor, King shot him in the forehead.

Drumm lifted sharply, discharged the other shotgun barrel into the new oak steps, and wheeled over backward to fling down the stairs. Though he was dead in his tracks, his feet found the steps for a moment before he fell, almost standing, to bounce at the landing and crash through the south window. King heard his body thump onto the lawn.

"Who's shooting who?" Buck Parnell cried out. His heavy steps came clanking along the lower hallway until he hit the stairs and came up them two at a time to the landing.

King could see nothing of him but the feather at the top of his hat.

King's right arm and leg were beginning to hurt down to the bone. He gritted his teeth, tried to keep his eye on the dancing feather below, and cocked his pistol again. He'd lost count, but he thought he had at least a couple of shots left. It didn't matter. If Buck came at him, one was all he'd ever get to use.

But Buck had stopped on the landing. "What's happened here?" Buck called out the empty window. "Why hell." He pointed his pistol down at an angle and fired twice. Then he ran back down the stairs and along the hall to the door King had entered. "Eli!" Buck was shouting, "Stop him, Eli! He's on the damned ladder! Get him, get him! Here he comes, Eli!"

Then he slammed into the locked door, bounced back, cursed it roundly, and fumbled with the bolt.

Chapter 28

December 8, 1894

Eli Parnell shivered. A cold wind cut through his coat right to the unvarnished hickory of his arms and chest. He leaned his wicked little short-barreled Greener into the angle made by the steps and the east wall of the courthouse. There in the darkness he tried again to make some sort of peace with God.

Eli had never wanted to kill anyone. He'd made no secret of that. But the others had forced him. He knew it; they knew it.

"Oh God," Eli murmured, "Thou knowest that I never wanted any part in taking any human life." But it seemed to Eli that a voice answered him immediately, a voice he had called up but had certainly not expected to hear. *Eli Parnell,* the voice said, *hypocrite and liar.* "Yes, Lord!" *You say that you never wanted to take another mortal's life?* "Lord, Thou knowest —" *I know. Twenty-five years ago you coveted another man's wife.* "She was older, but so beautiful! And unhappy! Lord, is there no end to thy vengeance?" *And did you not seek for the life of Dallas Castleberry?* "Oh God, Thou knowest I did!" *On thy knees for thy sins!*

Eli Parnell went to his knees like a felled buffalo, his hands flat together like shingles in front of his face, his lips moving without sound. "Yes Lord, I remember. My memory is never free of those things. But must I remember always as well the moment when Castleberry came right into my store and accused me concerning his wife and faced me down with a gun so that I've never been able again to walk with pride in this town, though no man knows my shame? Oh God, can Thou by no means separate me from the sins of my memory and set me in the quiet empty peaceful room of thy grace? Oh Dear God, may I please at the least make peace with my brother Buck and set him free of those desires which torment him!"

Eli spoke within his soul words he'd never found before, words he was certain God would accept. But he had hardly begun on the catalog of his sins when the first shotgun blast roared down through the skylight in the judge's office.

He sprang up, grabbing for the Greener. "Buck!" he cried, fearing in his newly warmed soul for his brother whose post was within the tower of Babel Eli had helped to build. "Buck!"

Eli used the brand-new shotgun to pull himself out from the courthouse wall to the bottom of the outside stairs. Fearfully, he took hold of the stone railing and started to climb the steps.

Already there had been another two shots, perhaps more. Eli wasn't counting. He was paddling up the stairway slower and slower as his heart bumped faster and louder with every step. Halfway up, at the landing, he dragged down to a stop like a fine draft horse pulling against a wagon brake. There he stood, bent at a sharp angle from the waist, panting with no control over the spasms, leaning against the crutch he'd made of the Greener. Somewhere behind and below him a woman was calling his name. Her shoes rang on the cold hard street. More guns went off inside the courthouse.

Then he heard Buck's voice. "Eli!" Buck screamed. "Stop him, Eli!"

"Eli!" the woman cried at the same time, drowning whatever else Buck was yelling. "Oh Eli, no! Don't! You can't!" Her steps by that time were clapping along the stone walkway toward the steps where Eli stood fixed, perhaps dying. He could not tell. He knew only that his chest hurt like a great throbbing bad tooth.

But the voice, the woman. It was his Sheila. Imagine. She calling his name for the whole town to hear. A harsh kind of pride swept through his wooden frame, straightened him to his full height, filled him with the strength of determination.

"Here he comes, Eli!" Buck shouted. Of course. This was the moment that God had prepared for Eli Parnell, the moment of triumph to be witnessed by his wife and his brother, the two most important people in the world. The only two people in the world for him.

Ten feet above Eli, someone was unbolting the great door. Eli knew that it was the Ranger, Jeff King, the one who threatened to ruin them all, the one who would kill Buck unless Eli faced down his own fear and acted. With a strong wooden thumb, he cocked both hammers on the Greener. Again he heard Buck's voice urging him to stop the fleeing Ranger. He knew that Buck was still alive. The joy of that realization warmed Eli's soul, gave him courage.

"Wait, Eli!" Sheila Parnell screamed. She was on the stone stairs at last, racing frantically from step to step. Somewhere inside the building Buck was calling. His voice echoed in her ears so forcefully that she thought he was calling her name. *Sheila,* he seemed to say, *Oh Sheila, darling Sheila, I'm ready to take you away!*

And then the door opened at the top of the stairs. Buck came dashing through it. She thought she saw his love flicker in his eye, a reflection of herself shutting everything else from his vision. At the same time she saw Eli lifting his arms, pointing a nasty black gun straight up at his brother. She screamed. "Noooooooooo!" But in that long heartbeat she knew Buck could never get out of the way. She knew Eli did not see well enough to recognize his own brother in time. She knew she and Buck were never going to board that train for California. "Buck!" she cried. "I love you!" But, as in a nightmare, no one heard her.

Eli saw the figure of King above him, a lean strong man with a pistol shining in his hand. But Eli was his match. Eli was as much a man as King. The shotgun said so. He pulled the front trigger, felt the wicked recoil smack him back against the wall and almost over it, but he had staggered King, stopped him in his tracks.

"No, not Buck!"

Eli heard Sheila's voice in his ear, but the words made no sense to him. She grabbed at his arm. He pushed her aside, wondering that she should try to spoil the moment. Getting the gun back into line, he pulled at the other trigger. The figure above him slammed backward against the tall wooden door, hung there in momentary crucifixion, then slid down it leaving a bright smear as it fell face forward on the cold stones. Sheila wailed like a hurt animal, pushed off him, and ran up the rest of the stairs.

"Oh Blessed Mary! Oh my Buck!" was the last thing he heard her say. And then she knelt beside the bloody mess of King's body, her voice shapeless.

Someone was running across the south lawn away from the courthouse, running with a queer, lurching, broken gait. Someone else making more noise was running toward it. Eli had the brief thought that all of them were folk in his dream. Then Buck walked out the door to stand a moment looking down at Sheila and King.

Eli could tell by the way that his one arm hung

that Buck was hurt. Hurt but not killed. Hurt but going to live! Buck stepped around the two on the stone floor and came down the steps to Eli. And when he came right up to Eli and took the Greener out of his hardwood hands, Buck had become Jeff King in Eli's dream.

King broke open the shotgun, threw away the smoking black hulls, and went on down the steps without a word. "But oh my Dear God," Eli prayed, "if that is King, then who lies dead on the floor above me? Who lies dead by my hand and mourned by my wife!"

Slowly, Eli Parnell sank to his knees on the cold stone of the landing and put the hickory palms of his hands over his ears lest he hear again that voice which waited to answer his question.

Chapter 29

December 8–9, 1894

Jeff King saw at a glance that Buck was dead. He turned his attention to Eli Parnell who still held a gun, but the elder brother stood stunned as if a cannon shell had gone off too near to him. King watched him closely as he came down the steps toward the landing.

Eli's eyes were glazed over. King did not believe that the merchant even saw him. Seeing no other weapon on the older man, King took the Greener away from him. Parnell made no effort to keep the shotgun, did not seem even to notice that it was gone.

King heard people running, but their faces were hazy and indistinct. He stumbled at the foot of the stairs and would have fallen if Higginbotham had not met him there with a steadying hand. The butcher stared up at the tableau on the steps.

"The rest of them inside?" the old man asked.

"Pretty much."

"You need to get that arm seen to." Higginbotham put out a hand to stop the first of the saloon crowd about to tackle the steps. "Hey, you, Rafe. You go find the doctor. Tom, go tell Felder. The rest of you just wait." He took up a position on the second step. "None of you is going up there to bother those people."

King was glad to see Higginbotham take hold. He steadied himself, standing alone. With his left hand, he lifted the Greener in tribute or farewell. "Listen," he said. "You got any buckshot shells for sale?"

"No," Higginbotharn said, "I don't. Not to you. But you can help yourself to a box of them under my main counter."

"Get a boy to bring my horse from the livery."

"Listen, you ain't going anywhere like that. You need a doctor."

King started for the store. "Get my horse," he repeated.

Higginbotham stared after him. "All right. But I'm getting the doctor first." He called one of the crowd up to him, deputized him into the unofficial new local government, told him where to send the doctor, and left him to guard the stairs.

Then he caught up with King. Taking him by his good arm, he led him across toward his store. "Hell," he said. "Come on. I'll show you. But I don't see what you want with ammunition now the battle's finished. What you need worse'n you know is some medical attention."

"No time."

"Time? Oh that's good. *'No time!'* We'll carve that on your stone." Inside the store he got King to sit down and yield up his right arm for inspection. "And what were you in such a rush about?"

"I promised a young woman I'd come for her when this was finished."

Ten minutes later the doctor tapped at Higginbotham's door. "Hig?"

"Come on in, Doc."

The doctor was a lean, bony, elderly man with a wispy goatee. He shook Higginbotham's hand and peered nearsightedly into the store. "Where's the patient?"

"Setting right here bleeding all over my counter."

"Great God, what'd you do to him? Run over him with the rolling harrow?"

"Buckshot."

The doctor clicked open his bag and began to set out shiny tools. "Hear there's a lot of it going around," he said. "I don't get much of that business, ordinarily. Seems like Felder ends up with most of those."

"Felder's across the street at the courthouse. Now let's see if you can keep this one away from him."

"Okay. Yes, most of him. Hope you weren't right-handed."

King raised his head, suddenly concerned. "Listen."

"Hey. I'm just funning you. Here, let me have a better look at that hand. A couple of shot went clean through. One small bone broken. Now the thing is we'll want to get the rest of these shot out."

"Later on."

"Not if you want to grow old using this arm and this leg."

King managed a short laugh. "It may not be necessary, then," he said. "Just wrap something around my arm and let me be on my way."

King struck the main DC ranch road and passed through the barred gate onto Castleberry land. The high clouds he'd seen earlier were gone now, carried east by the wind, so that moonlight whitened the road in front of him and threw harsh shadows among the brush to either side. Away from the town lights, a broad sweep of stars filled the southern sky.

King rode with head bowed, Eli's stubby shotgun across the saddle in front of him, his mind and body wrapped in fatigue and pain and bitter resolve. But it didn't matter. His horse had learned the road. They made it along at a speed which King figured would fetch him up at the ranch house a while before dawn. He couldn't be sure of it, but he thought that he had no vaquero escort. In fact, he had the feeling that the whole ranch had drawn up around its headquarters like a singed spider.

He was right.

Every hitchrail was full. Men and horses stood everywhere. King rode straight on along the main road until he approached the house. The vaqueros and workers reminded him of a hive of bees swarming. He knew every eye was on him as he reined his horse to a stop short of the porch.

Diana Castleberry stepped outside to put two more eyes on King. She was dressed again in her black riding clothes.

A black leather gunbelt around her waist held up a shining ivory-handled pistol. She stopped at the porch rail, tense and poised like a huntress sighting her prey.

Jeff King paid no more attention to the rest of the armed camp. He kept his eyes on the huntress. Of them all gathered about him, she was the only one who mattered. "Diana," he said.

She shook her head. "Not just now," she told him. "Go on up and see Papa first. After that I'll listen."

He thought he saw just the hint of a smile at the edges of her mouth. "Where is he?"

"Up on the hill."

He told his horse with his knees. He passed three or four worker bees standing in the road where the swarm had left them. They made no move to block his way, but stared up at him with a quiet sort of hunger he didn't much like. The horse started, then waited for the men to move. They didn't. King spoke to the horse.

The roan lifted his head and showed just a rim of white at the tops of his eyes. Then he whinnied sharply and walked up the road through the men. They moved. One of them reached out toward the stirrup. King put his bandaged right hand across the neck of the little Greener and dragged back both hammers with a double snap. It was enough.

For the first few steps he wondered if he would get a dozen bullets in his back. Then he put it out of his mind and concentrated on what waited for him at the top of the hill.

What waited was a tall and white old man who had lost his hat. Dallas Castleberry stood in the little cemetery covered by the daybright moon with the fine shadows of winter oak branches.

King left his horse at the low iron gate out of respect for the dead. He got down with some difficulty, cradling the Greener across his chest. Only then did he realize how stiffly painful his whole right side had become. It showed in his gait as he came through the brittle grass toward the new grave and Castleberry.

The rancher stood, leaning heavily on the tall double stone which held Emma's name and his own. His right hand held a glinting-new shotgun in balance atop the stone and pointing generally in King's direction. A dark thumb-wide rivulet of blood trickled down across his belt to pool blackly op top of the stone.

"I can hear you from there," he said to the Ranger. His voice was thick and throaty. The little puddle of blood found its way past some unseen dam and spilled to run down the front of the tombstone and lose itself in the *C* of the word *Castleberry*.

You can see me better if I don't come closer, King

thought. He didn't care. He was close enough. "I didn't want to think it was you on that roof tonight. But it had to be. Nobody else knew."

"Didn't you think I could climb that high?"

"I'm here to arrest you."

"Hoop!" Castleberry said. In better times it would have been a laugh. A little bit of blood showed at the edge of his mouth. "No need to keep looking behind you. I've given all of them their orders to stay down there and leave this to you and me. If there's shooting and you ride back down, they're to let you pass. Hoop. But was I you in that case, I'd head on south to the next county before I turned east again."

"I have to arrest you because you killed the judge."

"Hoop. Glad to hear that, anyway. You taken to arresting people for killing vermin?"

"There's been a world of men arrested for killing vermin. Laws against it. But I guess a worse thing was killing Cy Timm. I could arrest you for that, too."

"Suit yourself."

"And for shooting Crow."

The rancher stirred, bending his head to peer at King. "What're you talking about? Crow was my ears." His voice grew stronger, indignant. "Is he dead? Who'd do a thing like that?"

"That's what I said about Timm. I figured the judge or one of his folk for a cowardly act like that. It wouldn't have figured that a big brave man like you —"

"Watch your tongue!" Castleberry snapped. He was leaning more heavily on the stone now, the barrels of the shotgun angled more sharply at King. "Don't wag it at me or — at that poor little bastard Timm. He was a gamecock. But you don't want to arrest me for him. The judge either. You wouldn't have rid through all them vaqueros to arrest me for those two."

"You're mistaken."

"No. Hoop." It wasn't a laugh any more. He was trying to swallow back the blood. "If you're going to try to arrest me, arrest me for killing your bushwhacking brother."

"You did that too?" King's voice went hard and he leaned a little toward the grave where Castleberry stood.

" 'I take pen in hand,' hoop!" he said. " 'To ask you to dispatch a force of Rangers to arrest the murderer of Sheriff Hollis.' "

"Yes," King said. "The judge had figured that out. You wrote that letter."

"Hoop. On the roof again. Heard their plan. Saw Timm draw the black bean. Knew he'd never get the job done. Shot Hollis before they could make another plan. Knew the letter would bring the Rangers down on them." He stopped and swallowed. "Never expected somebody like you."

"Why Timm?"

"Bring them down on you. Ask them about the black bean, is any of them left."

King took a step nearer, shifting to ease the

pull of the Greener. "Funny thing," he said. "The rest of it fits, but not Hollis. You told me you didn't kill him, early on. I believed you."

"Got — you — there — hooo—" Leaning into the stone to hold himself up, Dallas Castleberry reached across with his left hand to set the hammers on his new shotgun.

"Don't do that," King said.

"Ride — south," Castleberry said.

He was just beginning to bring the gun barrels to bear on King when the Ranger tripped both triggers on the Greener. The recoil battered his hand and arm viciously, and he went to his knees from the sudden shock. Chips of marble flew from the tombstone below and around Castleberry. King saw Castleberrry's bright new barrels tilt straight up into the sky, driving smoke and flame toward the moon. He did not walk to the stone to see what two charges of buckshot had done. He knew.

All during the long minute it took him to drag himself up into his saddle, King was thinking about the ride south and away from a yard full of swarming bees waiting to see who had won the duel. He turned the roan, reining short for a moment to look at the bell tower of the chapel just outside the fence.

For an instant, he remembered shelter, pelting rain outside, warmth and yielding softness, black hair against his cheek, black eyes wide and shining. Then he shook his head. The rain was gone, and the bell tower stood sharp and clear against cold stars. King broke open the Greener, fed it two more big bites of death, and turned his horse back along the road toward the DC headquarters.

Chapter 30

December 9, 1894

Jeff King let the shotgun rest across his lap while he drew his long heavy rifle out of the scabbard with his left hand. He levered a cartridge into the chamber, set the hammer on safe, and slid the long gun back into the boot. Even if he'd had full use of his right hand, he figured the chances were pretty slim that he would live long enough to use the rifle. But it never hurt to be ready.

Sooner than he expected it, the horse came to the edge of the mesa and started picking its way down the steep road toward the headquarters. King spent that last minute thinking how it might have been for him if he hadn't been driven to kill Dallas Castleberry.

He would be riding up to the front door to ask for Diana's hand, to put her in her little buggy, tie the twin sorrel ponies on behind, take her away with him. They would take the train to St. Louis or Chicago or somewhere really nice for their honeymoon. He spent one last moment thinking about the afternoon with her in the little chapel on the hill. He thought of the way that hard rain had slanted against the tiny stained-glass windows outside. He remembered the smell of her hair, the fairness of her skin at her throat, the frailness of her body once one got past the fury of her spirit.

Would she really have married him? Could they have been happy, even if he had not known what he knew now?

But he wasn't ready to think about what he knew now. That would come soon enough. Maybe — if he hadn't known what he knew — they would have married, would have taken the ponies to Waxahachie where he would have introduced Diana to his sister-in-law and his nephews. But of course. Diana already knew them and they already knew her. And King already knew what he knew. And in the middle of all those thoughts of what might have been loomed the ghosts of C.D. Hollis and Dallas Castleberry.

King damned it all to hell, laid back the hammers of the Greener, and rode on down into the valley of the shadow of death. Seventy yards away but clear in the dying moonlight, Constanzo Alvarez walked across the through road leading two fat ponies. King could make out the two new small saddles on their backs. Alvarez led the ponies up to the house and tied them off at the porch rail.

For a last moment, King pictured Diana in a white lacy dress, running to meet him, forgiving him for everything, smiling at King, calling out his name as she came.

Chapter 31

December 9, 1894

"King!" Diana Castleberry shouted at him. "Jeff King! Here!"

As he came even with the house, King saw her on the porch alone, standing just where she'd been before he started up to the mesa top. Straight across the road two vaqueros sat their horses easily, watching. King had first seen Saul and Octavio flanking Dallas Castleberry; now they guarded the new mistress of the DC. The rest of the area was as empty as if God had come with a great broom and swept away every other living thing.

King turned his back on the vaqueros and rode his horse right up to the porch. For a long moment the man and woman stared into each other's eyes. King saw in her eyes that she knew he had killed her father and that she would hate him for it ten years past the end of time. Like so many things, it didn't matter so much now.

"Where did you get the shotgun?" he asked.

Diana Castleberry did not smile, but she let her teeth show as a hunting lioness might. "This

292

one?" She lifted the slender, long barreled bird gun she held.

King shook his head the slightest bit. "Listen," he said. "I can see most of it now. I understand how you came in the night Hollis was killed. You were on the ten-fifty train. You got off without anybody seeing you while it was waiting on the siding for the eastbound express. But where'd you get the shotgun?"

Her expression didn't change. "I brought it home from Springfield, Massachusetts." She spoke lightly, as if the matter were no longer important. "I was in school there. I'd bought it as a present for Papa."

Jeff King wished he'd been wrong. He wished Dallas Castleberry hadn't tried to lead him off the track by taking the blame on himself. If Castleberry hadn't overplayed his hand, King would never have understood that it had to be Diana. He wished she had lied to him. Then he could have let it all go. But of course it didn't matter. Whatever she said and whatever she felt, there could be nothing for them now.

He glanced away from her at the waiting vaqueros. It had been easy to ride into the DC. Riding out of it now was somewhere on the far side of unlikely.

"Diana." He figured it would be the last time he'd speak her name. He said it softly and gently. "Guess we've made a pretty good mess of it from start to finish, haven't we?"

"I did what I had to do — I killed my brother's

killer. You meant to do the same. Maybe you still do."

"If you'd told me earlier —" King let that go.

Diana might have read his thoughts. "It doesn't matter." She lifted the barrels of the shotgun. Desperation was in her face and her voice. "You've killed Papa, but you won't kill the DC. You won't live to arrest me."

"Are you going to do it again?" King asked her. "You're the one who said I should let it end. Did you really mean to go away with me?"

"Oh, Jeff, yes!" The cry burst from her, but the next second her face was cold and remote again. "That's over. Now you're a killer — and a Ranger — nothing more."

"I have a captain. Slater. If you kill me, he'll be next. He won't let it go either, not until he knows the truth."

She narrowed her eyes. "Are you just trying to save your life? What's better if I don't kill you?"

"Maybe you can see that the hammers are back on this Greener. I'll make a fight of it if I have to."

"I don't think you've got the stomach to shoot a woman — unless it runs in your family."

"Maybe not, but it could cost you a couple of good men. You were right to begin with. I'd rather let it end."

"How?" Her voice was sharp and suspicious. Across the road, the two gunmen stirred and moved a little farther apart. "How can it now? After all that's happened."

King drew a breath deep enough to hurt his side. "End it. That's all. I ride out, forget what I could never prove anyway. You keep this ranch that means more to you than anything else."

"There was a time when you meant —"

"No there wasn't," King cut in roughly. "All of that was built on a lie. There was never any way for us. And there's no way now. The choice is to kill another time, or just to cut our losses and let it end."

The moon caught a glint in her eye. It might have been a tear of anger. It might have been anything. "And your brother?"

"He's dead. I can't bring him back, no more than you can your father. And I don't want to kill anybody else." He watched her for a moment, then lifted the Greener clear with his left hand and dropped it in the road. "Let it be, Diana. Stop here. You'll have the ranch."

She stared at him for a space that seemed endless while he waited for a bullet from her riders or a blast from the gun she held. Then, slowly, she let the bird gun's barrels droop toward the floor of the porch and her thin shoulders shook with a racking sob.

"Go on, then. Ride out loose and free. Go free wherever you'd like the rest of your life. I'll have the ranch!"

He nodded. He understood that no one responsible for such a ranch as the DC would ever be free. He turned the horse and started out of the yard.

She called to the vaqueros in Spanish. King understood enough of it to know that they wouldn't shoot unless they went against her orders. "You, King," she said.

He looked back over his shoulder.

"You take these damned worthless twin ponies with you, hear? I don't want them on the place."

He untied their reins, looped them over his saddle horn, and rode out at a slow enough pace. When he topped the hill toward Willow Springs, he paused a moment to wipe his brow against the rising sun. Then he turned to look a final time at the DC. The last thing he saw was three riders, their shadows, long and spindly in the first sunlight, going slowly up the mesa trail toward the old cemetery. The leader, a small figure in black, paused a moment and King saw a white face turned his way. He started to wave, thought better of it, and rode north to lie to Captain Slater.